The Girvin Social Club

BY
Guy Mills

Marble Press
New York, New York

The Girvin Social Club

BY

Guy Mills

Photos on front and back covers by Guy Mills

Copyright 2007 by Guy Mills

ISBN 978-1-4276-1214-4

Marble Press
130 Church Street, Suite 273
New York, New York 10007

Printed in the United States of America

**Dedicated to
Kelly and Joe**

The Girvin Social Club

TABLE OF CONTENTS

CHAPTER ONE

Damascus, Syria

THE SYRIAN HEAT! The only word that came to mind was...oppressive. Ashur was uncomfortable. The heat was becoming unbearable, even for a young man born in the "oasis" city of Damascus where humidity and heat were a part of daily life. He had only recently returned from a half dozen years of schooling in the United States, at the full expense of a group of mentors who paid the way for many young Syrians to be educated in the West, and he was spoiled.

Now, he waited outside the unassuming mud hut with his two most trusted friends— his cousins, Said and Samir. Even though they had all grown up in Syria together, he had become soft after leaving his home for so many years, and he could feel it. They were all in their twenties, at the prime of life. But somehow, his cousins seemed so much stronger. He knew that they were both highly trained in guerilla warfare, and that they had been there/done that. He hadn't. He worried if they thought him to be weak...or if they could see the weakness he felt in himself. Said and Samir had picked him up at the airport just a week ago, and they quickly informed him that they had been given the honor of joining him in this mysterious adventure, wherever it might take them. They had been more than willing to agree, as they knew it was for a just cause, regardless of what they were about to be asked to do.

A part of Ashur flat-out ached for the pleasant air conditioning he had become so completely accustomed to in Texas. The basalt desert of South Syria was known for the intensity of its heat. The rare slices of shade in the dusty streets offered little comfort or relief. The Syrian sun seemed to bear down on him without mercy. There was not the slightest breath of air movement, other than the brief, hot, swish from a passing car or truck. The air smelled foul from exhaust fumes, sour sweat reeking from passersby, and from rank, shallow, sewers stagnating nearby that were overwhelmed with floating decayed food and human filth—all only a few meters away. There was no escape, nor was there complaint from his cousins. Ashur kept his thoughts to himself, but it was a far cry from 6th Street he loved so much in downtown Austin. And, he was far from the young woman who had introduced him to the good life in the United States.

Soon he would meet inside the hut with a small, and very elite, group of wealthy Sunni bazaar merchants, the ulama, who summoned him home for a purpose yet to be revealed to him or to his companions. Ashur had been called by these powerful men to Damascus to return a great favor, and ulama favors had to be returned to avoid the harshest of penalties. He owed them his years in the United States and his American education. And, they had made small payments to his parents in his absence as a sort of tribute for the "borrowing" of their son.

The wait seemed an eternity. The heat, the stench, and the tension were working on his nerves. Impatience was welling up in him; but just as he thought he could wait no longer before imploding, the door to the hut opened and a dark hand reached through a shadowed space and motioned for Ashur to enter. Said and Samir had sat down on the ground resting their backs against the warm shaded wall of the building while Ashur nervously paced back and forth in front of them, kicking up bits of dust with his sandals that blew towards his friends.

Samir looked up as Ashur turned toward the door, waving the dust away, and advised, "Patience is a virtue, Ashur. Show them you are a patient man. Show your inner strength." They knew him too well, even in his absence. That's the way of it, with close friends—they understand, thought Ashur.

As he stepped through the doorway, Ashur's eyes struggled to find their focus. The room he entered had very little light. There was a strong musty and sour odor that made his stomach turn, adding to his nervousness. He took a couple of steps toward the table and stood stone still as someone closed the heavy wooden door behind him. Momentarily, his gaze drew downward toward a small table. His vision gradually adjusted to the light, and he soon could see three men seated around the table. They were all staring at him with grim expressions that warned of heavy words soon to come. He felt the sickening feeling in the pit of his stomach growing, as much from anticipation of the unknown as from fear.

The heaviest of the men rose from his seat and began talking, breaking the uncomfortable silence.

"We need your services now, Ashur." The speaker was clearly the great, most learned, and unquestionably respected alim that Ashur had only seen once years ago, but the man was exactly the same as he remembered. He was a man to be obeyed without question. "The cost of your American education these past years has been high, and the time has come for you to repay your debt to us. We call upon you now to perform a task of supreme importance to your people and more important—to Allah and to the Jihad."

The alim paused, with a look of deep concern crossing his brow, to drink slowly from a dark-stained tankard.

Wild thoughts raced through Ashur's mind as he imagined multiple possibilities, one after another, in rapid succession. Did they want someone killed? Was he to be an assassin? Were they sending him into Iraq...or Afghanistan to fight? Would there be a mission that involved some clandestine spying operation...maybe in Israel? He quickly dismissed most of his thoughts as a bit outrageous, but Ashur assumed he was about to be given some compelling, and possibly dangerous, responsibility. His instincts told him to prepare. It was definitely pay-back time.

The moment of silence seemed like an eternity, and then the alim collected himself and spoke once again.

"We want you to go back to the United States. You have fresh knowledge of the Americans and of Texas. We have selected you to lead a special mission. We expect you to reap Allah's vengeance upon the American in such a way that they have never seen before, and a way that they will never forget. We want you to change the future, Ashur. Syria will soon rise to meet a new level of power and influence, not only in the Middle East, but throughout the world. You will be Allah's instrument. We will give you the weapons and fighters to accomplish the mission. Will you do this for us?"

With words breaking from his dry throat, Ashur replied. "It would be my duty and my honor to serve you and our people." He said what he thought must be said.

The alim stood and pointed to two wooden boxes stacked in the corner of the room. They were small, vintage suitcases, yellowed and bruised from age. It was clear they had been used a great deal.

A second seated man spoke and said, "Those boxes contain what are known as improvised nuclear devices."

Ashur felt the hair on the back of his neck stand up, and his chest began pounding. So many thoughts flashed though his mind. He wondered if he was as afraid as he felt he was, and he wondered if they could see the fear in him. He wondered to if he had the courage and skill to do whatever it was they expected him to do with those "devices." He wondered if he could meet their expectations well enough. Mostly, Ashur wondered if he would survive beyond the mission. It was all to be done for the Jihad and for Allah...and for Syria...and ultimately to keep his family safe, wasn't it? Ashur knew that if he refused, his family would suffer immediate consequences. He knew his own people were ruthless and quick to reap vengeance. He also knew that even a look of hesitation would be likely to abruptly end his own existence.

Ashur knew he was being closely observed and possibly more closely listened to by the men in that room. So, he was careful to 'sound' the way he knew he had to sound. Refusal was out of the question, but all his instincts told Ashur to run. He didn't.

The seated man went on. "Small as they may appear, those boxes contain the materials needed to do incredibly serious and long-lasting damage where ever they are exploded. You should know that they were both purchased, with great expense, from rebels in Chechnya a few years ago. The rebels had actually built three suitcase sized dynamite/cesium bombs with the intention of causing political and economic destabilization among their Russian enemies. Fortunately for us, they failed in an attempt to explode one of those bombs in Moscow's Izmailovo Park in 1996. They decided to market the remaining two bombs to generate money to fund other anti-Russian ventures. We were most fortunate to come in contact with the rebel leadership when we did and to procure the weapons. The purchase, and subsequent movement of the weapons to Damascus went entirely un-noticed and we believe the bombs are now forgotten, for all practical purposes."

Again, a silence ensued that seemed to last light-years. Ashur had heard of the "dirty bomb" from news reports over his years living in the United States. He was aware of the fear across the globe that existed for those kinds of weapons. He suddenly recalled a recent news release that made the Associated Press and the New York Times that the US Government Accountability Office had managed to sneak, completely unchallenged, a small quantity of nuclear waste across the Mexican border into Texas. They did it not only once, but several times over a span of a few months. He wondered if the United States had yet taken any action to prevent this from happening, for real, in the future.

He seriously doubted it. His time in the United States had given him insight. Americans talk, and they talk, and they talk. The leaders in Washington, and in Texas, used their political rhetoric to gain votes, and they just seemed to talk even more during election years. Seldom, if ever, was there genuine action. Ashur knew the border between Mexico and the United States in Texas was essentially open to anyone with the nerve and guile to sneak in. The border, as the enemies of Allah on Fox News liked to say, was incredibly "porous" in nature. It was essentially an open border for anyone who wanted badly enough to cross it.

The alim spoke once again, seeming to know exactly what Ashur was thinking. "The United States cannot act to effectively defend its own borders. Surely you know this from your experiences in Texas. The endless debate rages in Washington, as their Washington Post newspaper tell us. And, we watch it on CNN every day. Don't their politicians know we watch? Do they think we are so ignorant? We know they can't decide what measures might be taken to better secure their own borders. Some want to build a wall. Others want to build miles and miles of fence. Some think they need more Border Patrol and Customs personnel. Others think they need more aerial surveillance. Now the talk is about sending their National Guard to watch the border but the states have sent only a handful of soldiers. The states are not cooperating as expected. The Americans are over-committed in Iraq and Afghanistan. They have worn out their military strength, and their morale amongst their troops is at an all-time low. The nation's leadership can't ever agree on what to do, so they do nothing at all. Eventually, they may compromise and send a token few more Guardsmen to the border. There will be so few that they will be easy to avoid."

He continued, "The fact is that the United States has thousands of miles of border between Mexico, Canada, and itself, and the United States government is not only unable, but politically unwilling, to act to guarantee the safety of its own people. The handful of Border Patrol people, Customs officials, the "militia," and the few poorly manned Boarder Patrol Checkpoints simply cannot take care of their business with any degree of effectiveness. The border from Mexico into the United States is, at least for now, virtually unguarded and that gives us the perfect opportunity to take advantage of the situation if we act quickly."

The alim went on, "We have a window of time for this plan to work, if we can get moving before the border furor results in an outcry from the American public which forces the government to act. When that happens, there will eventually be more restriction. There is always the risk that American political expediency might actually cause something to be done. But we may have a brief window of time to duplicate their government's recent success in crossing the border with simulated nuclear weapons. The difference is that we will do it with real weapons and with determination and strength drawn directly from the will of Allah. Our intent is for you, with the help of a few others, to ignite these bombs in their oil and gas fields. We wish for you to cause as much long-term havoc as possible. To be honest, Ashur, it is possible that none of you will return, but you must know that you all will be martyrs and you will be remembered as heroes for generations among our people. In the name of Allah and the Jihad!"

One of the seated men who was totally unfamiliar to Ashur positioned himself to speak. He was a very dark complexioned, heavily bearded man in his 50's. "Boy, we want you to travel to Mexico immediately. We have strong contacts there and we have already made arrangements for you to be supplied and transported. In addition to your cousins, we have two very experienced fighters—my daughters, in fact—to send along with you. One of them has excellent experience with explosives and has been fully briefed on how to use our special weapons. They will meet you and your cousins in Mexico with the suitcases. Then, we want you to take your team and make your way to the border and cross into Texas. Based on our intelligence, and with the support of the cartel, we believe crossing the border will be a relatively easy task, Ashur. Now, beneath the desert of the West Texas Permian Basin lies a very large portion of the United States' oil and gas reserve – it is thought to be as much as 25% of the nation's petroleum holdings, and it is all produced in a relatively small area. We are going to place tremendous trust in you by giving you responsibility for these weapons. They cannot be lost or wasted! You will have only one chance. We expect you to explode the two radiological devices in those strategic oil and gas fields. In doing so, you will strike a crippling blow to the American economy for many years to come. Your actions will effectively debilitate their civil authority and their military. More so, you will disrupt even the most mundane everyday travel of the citizens in their country. We also believe this action, when effectively implemented, will cause widespread chaos and riots, and that this will give us additional opportunities to take advantage of the soft Americans. But most importantly, young man, you will create a lasting panic and lingering fear that will remain as a constant terror in the minds of the American people. The explosion of these little bombs will create an invisible and deadly fear they've never experienced before, and they will be afraid for a very long time to come!"

CHAPTER TWO

Girvin, Texas

PEOPLE WHO KNOW West Texas know that Girvin is "just a spit" south of Odessa, and thirty miles northeast of Fort Stockton. It is a very small town of a size and condition not unusual for this part of the state. The population is often fluid, dependent entirely upon the needs of the oil and gas production facilities in the area. In fact, since 9/11, the population had grown from a dozen or so hardy residents to several times that number. The town had been accused lately by the local daily Odessa American of being a "ghost town," but it really wasn't. Most of the current residents were roughnecks who worked the oil and gas fields. They lived in a variety of dilapidated mobile homes in the desert surrounding the town. Unfortunately, or maybe fortunately, there weren't many places for the roughnecks to play.

The center of Girvin happens to be the Social Club—the Girvin Social Club, to be exact. The Social Club is a beat-up old cantina on the main blacktop, U.S. Highway 385, running through town. The Club offers a single, very filling, evening meal and it is a great place to have a cold beer or two at the end of a dry West Texas day. Passing motorists not familiar with the area seldom stop since they think the Social Club is an abandoned building from its run-down appearance—with loose boards, cracked glass, and a half-dozen broken down vehicles, rusted, without windshields or wheels, rotting alongside the ragged chain link fencing bordering the property. The fact is that pretty much only the locals knew it existed as the lone refuge for thirsty and hungry folks in the northern range of the Chihuahuan Desert. Another thing was for sure: it was only after dark that the building truly came alive.

Molly Mason had been bartending and cooking at the Social Club since the current petroleum boom began four or five years ago. She was raised in Crane, a few miles to the north. She graduated from high school, took a few classes at a nearby junior college in Odessa, and then met someone who quickly and mercilessly broke her heart. She fled to Girvin and took over the "management" of the Social Club. The roughnecks knew Molly was one tough lady. She ran a tight ship and kept the boys in line with relative ease. Some say that if she were to ever clean herself up, she'd be quite a catch. One thing for sure, she was a handsome woman. The first thing men noticed about her was her height. She was definitely tall, approaching 5'8" or more, and was even taller with her boots on. It wasn't hard for her to look most men directly in the eyes. Her dark hair was nearly always pulled back in a ponytail. She had a good figure, as the blue jeans and t-shirt she wore joined to reveal so clearly. She never wore makeup, but Molly didn't really need it. The fact was that these days men simply weren't in the cards for Molly. She'd sworn off them and was crystal clear about that with the men who tried her. They were the same men who totally relied on Molly for their evening meal and for the only feminine conversation around. With Molly, it was all business. They all soon accepted that—that is, all those except for Owen. There was something about Owen she liked, and he new it.

The labor intensive work in the oil and gas fields, for the most part, slows down a bit when darkness comes. And most evenings, all ten tables, plus the bar, in the Social Club are occupied. The oil and gas men are the "regulars." They come in, bone tired from the backbreaking work of the day, and look forward to Molly's home style cooking, followed by generally good natured laughter, loud talk, darts, pool, cards....but especially ice cold beer. Molly had an old horse-watering tank behind the bar that she kept full of ice and bottles of beer. After the typical West Texas day, the chilled brew in that tank was irresistible to the men.

There was no question that Owen was a

roughneck, through and through. He'd served three years in the Army, and spent a year of his military time helping to restore the damaged well sites in the oil fields of Iraq. On top of that, he was a Cajun from a poor, blue collar family in Louisiana. He was a self-made man, not rich by any measure, but he had come a long way in life using his mind and his backbone. He had moved to the Girvin area from New Orleans about two years earlier. He still carried a bit of an accent that exposed his background to those who listened or cared. He was a hard worker and he knew his business inside out. Now he was the driller and foreman for Carpenter Gas and Oil, and he supervised a crew of five men working the fields around Girvin. The crew was swamped with work with the current gas and oil boom. There seemed to be no end to it. The crew kept the machinery working and the gas and oil flowing. Owen had a fine crew. Each one of his people gave his all. Whatever it took, the crew could do it, and whatever they did they did better than anyone else.

Owen and the crew were in the Social Club practically every evening. It was their respite to those long days of constantly tasting the sandy grit of red West Texas dirt in their teeth, facing the howling winds, knowing up close and personal the incredible, parched dryness of the land. They were a close bunch, good friends who knew each other well enough to trust each other implicitly. They depended on one another every single day. And they respected each other. The "Carps" liked to have fun, and they liked the Social Club. Every now and then they fought and argued with one another, as much as brothers might occasionally do. But, there was a special bond between those men. It was a bond that came from standing shoulder to shoulder, day after day, working in difficult conditions. That bond kept them together, and sometimes even saved their lives.

Owen's crew was very young, men all in their twenties. Well, they were all young except for one man—Ralph Scott (Preacher they called him, or Preach). Ralph lectured the men more often than they cared to recall, and he earned his nickname honestly. A long, long time ago, he had been the minister of his own tiny wayward church. That life hadn't worked out so well, but he still had a habit of occasionally backsliding to quoting scripture in a way that sometimes annoyed the crew.

Owen always stood up for Preacher, even though his penchant for "preaching" to the younger guys seemed a bit hypocritical. The truth was that Ralph had sowed his share of wild oats. He liked the ladies and they liked him. It was a small problem with the wife of a congregation member that spoiled the ministerial gig. Preacher had even spent a short time in jail as a teenager for an indiscretion with an older neighbor's wife that had come to light in an unfortunate way. Mistakes were made. In fact, Preacher had found Jesus while he was in jail, so maybe it wasn't all bad for him. But his affinity for the 'weaker sex' was ever-present. Even now, in spite of the fact that Ralph was pushing 60, he had more than one woman chasing him. And, there was that javalina-of-a-woman "mudlogger" who was more than persistent in trying to win the man over, to the point of pure disgust, at least in Owen's mind. But, Ralph knew drilling equipment, pumps, hydraulics, gauges, and all sorts of machinery like no one else in the business. He was good at his job and Owen needed someone with Ralph's skills to keep things running. On top of that, Ralph was intensely loyal to Owen. Owen had given him a job when he couldn't get one. Ralph never forgot that. So, the two of them had a perfect understanding.

Each man on the crew had a nickname, as was the custom in the oil and gas fields in Texas. Most of the field workers didn't know each other's real names, since they usually heard only the nicks. The rest of the team included Sean Moore (Cowpaddy). Sean was about as "local" as they got, having grown up on a large ranch not far from Girwin. He loved to hunt, and was a dead shot with the jackrabbits and deer that roamed the ranch. He was also very good with horses. He'd even tried the rodeo circuit for a few months after leaving high school. He just wasn't good enough to compete consistently with the big boys. The crew often accused him, in their sick and generally off-color way, of missing the cows back on the ranch. Apparently from childhood on, Sean had a problem with stepping in every fresh cow pile in the country. He went through a lot of boots. And, in the heat, cow piles didn't stay fresh for long, so members of the crew often chided him for following the 'good lookin' cows around for totally indecent reasons. They like to point out that one cow or another seemed to "have eyes" for Sean. Otherwise, they teased, how would he have so much fresh shit on his boots? Simply put, cow piles were like magnets to Sean and his boots were usually splattered with cowshit. He earned his nickname well.

Then there was Roy Carpenter (Dinner Roll). Roy was about 5'4", and maybe 250 pounds. At 22, he was the youngest crew member. He was strong as an ox, as long as endurance wasn't an issue. He gained his moniker from the huge belly that hung over his big belt buckle like a giant slab of raw bread dough. Dinner Roll never seemed to get enough to eat. His pockets were always stuffed with food of some sort. He snacked on sweets incessantly. Unfortunately, his lunchbox was often the target of unpleasant practical jokes—ones that Dinner Roll seldom found to be funny, but jokes that the crew absolutely took delight in perpetrating. One time the boys put a couple of sand lizards in the box, closed it up tight, and sat it in the sun. Well, after a couple of hours in the triple-digit temperature, one could only imagine what the box smelled like – box fried lizard. At lunchtime, Dinner Roll discovered his lunch box had been moved from his shady storage place, so he was immediately suspicious from past experience. He opened the lid of the box anyway and when the first whiff of the contents hit him, he lost every little morsel he'd eaten that day. It wasn't a pretty sight, and it was bad enough for the crew that it was likely enough they'd never do that prank again. The funniest part of all was that the next day, Dinner Roll came to work with a huge chromium chain and padlock wrapped around his lunch box. After a few days, no one had touched his lunchbox. He figured his security measures had worked, but the fact was that no one wanted to see the contents of his stomach again. It was simply too much for them to stand.

Dinner Roll could do about any of the less challenging jobs on a rig. He was, as he liked to brag, "versatile." The fact was that he was so overweight that the heat wore him down too quickly. He gave up on the work that required anything but short physical exertion, and he gave up a little too easily. And he complained about work (and everything else) like there was no end to it. Owen often thought of replacing him, but Dinner Roll played his part just well enough to keep his job. He knew enough to stay just ahead of getting himself into trouble. He was clearly the weakest link on the crew. And there was also that ornery situation that it was Dinner Roll's mother, Janci, who owned Carpenter Gas and Oil.

Guy Carroll (Buster) was often the life of the party. Guy, mostly Irish, liked to fight and liked to drink. He was fearless, so much so that Owen wondered if he had a death wish. He was always the first to volunteer for the risky jobs. Guy often sported a black eye or bruised cheek gained from some unpleasant physical exchange. He never walked away from a fight. Preacher was always lecturing him about "turning the other cheek." That didn't work with Guy. He never quit. He never gave up. He was obsessive compulsive to a fault about his work. He'd spent time in Chicago before moving to Kansas City, and then to Texas. No one knew much about Guy, since he didn't talk about himself much. He was a private kind of man. One thing was for sure, though—trouble seemed to find him as easily as bad breath on an old dog. Owen had bailed him out of jail twice in the last six months for bar fights in Odessa. Owen tried his best to keep the crew around Girvin on the weekends for just that reason. Guy was a good crew member though, and was tough enough for the heaviest work. He was usually the last one to quit in the evening, and he never left any job undone that could be finished in the same day. Owen counted on Guy for that, and he gave him the most difficult, backbreaking, jobs to do, because he knew Guy would do them better than anyone else on the crew, and Guy never complained. He just did his job and did it well to the finish.

Finally, there was Darrell Garber (College Boy), who made it all the way to his senior year in mechanical engineering before dropping out to work in the gas fields to "save up a few bucks." Darrell was from Midland. He claimed to have known members of THE Bush family, but no one honestly believed him. He came from money, and drove expensive cars, one after another. He wasn't a good driver and no one who knew him would willingly ride with him. He seemed to habitually hit large, stationary objects with his cars, but he always managed to walk away from wrecks and collisions that would kill anyone else. He often said he planned to finish school someday, but no one believed him. The crew just wanted him to take driving lessons and slow down. He was good at fabrication and basic drilling problem solving – a good man to have on the crew, especially with the shortage of fully trained engineers. College Boy was … well, good enough, but they didn't let him drive.

All in all, they were a tight crew, bonded from so many days and nights of working together. They knew each other's weaknesses, to be sure, but they knew above all else they could count on each other when the chips were down and when a tough job needed to be done. There were no real slouches in this group. They pulled together. For some odd reason, only Owen didn't have a nickname. No one knew why that was the case, and no one had ever asked why not. He was clearly the driller and the crew's foreman. The crew liked him and they respected him. That was all that mattered.

CHAPTER THREE

Damascus International Airport

FADIA AND MONA had spent a hectic early morning packing their bags and trying to catch a taxi to the airport. They were traveling light, with only a carry-on canvas bag each. Both of them toted a canvas bag that contained a small wooden suitcase. Both women were anxious, but they didn't show it. Traveling from Damascus wasn't ever easy, especially given the fact that the Syrian Airline flights were consistently irregular, at best. They would not know if the flight to Ataturk would have enough passengers to make until the very last minute. They needed to get to Ataturk on time to catch another irregular flight on KLM to Madrid, and from there a Mexicana flight to Vera Cruz. A missed flight now would hold up the entire plan. They knew that they were to meet Ashur, Said, and Samir in two days in Vera Cruz, Mexico. Any delay in the timeline would put the project at risk. So they were nervous.

Fortunately, to their relief, the flight made and was on time. As they stood waiting, Mona looked at Fadia and said quietly, "Can we trust this boy, Ashur? Why would they pick someone so untried for to lead this mission? I don't understand. And the other two aren't much better."

Fadia glanced back and said, sharply, "We trust the alim and Allah. That's all we need to worry about. Yes, we do not know this boy, but Father says he comes from important lineage. And, he has a valuable American education that could serve us well. It is our role to help, no matter what the circumstances, and no matter who has been given leadership. We will not let this mission fail. It will all take care of itself. It is intended that we go and we will do our part, whatever is asked of us and regardless of what we have to do. We will make sure the mission is successful. They are ready to board us, so quit talking."

The boarding line moved forward. Carry-on bags were rarely searched and Mona and Fadia got on the plane with no issues. They found seats in the rear and kept their deadly baggage in their laps. Security was, at best, lax. Damascan electronic airport screening typically failed to pick up anything less than a very, very large metal object. There were only random searches, and those could be "excused" for a price. If they were stopped, the women were prepared to pay as much money as it took to buy the blindness of the boarding agents. Test travelers had already conducted checks at Ataturk and Madrid just two weeks earlier, and those checks had proven the same security system faults existed in both of those airports. The results of those tests were accurate.

The two women were veterans of the "insurgency" in Iran. Both had been trained for many months by Iranians at a secret Al Qaeda camp in eastern Syria. Even though they were blood sisters, they had become even closer in the camp, and that closeness had carried them both through the stress and hazards of dangerous street fighting in Mosul and Kirkuk. They had fought hard, as hard as the Syrian and Iranian men. They had maimed men and taken lives, not only from the despised "Americanized" Iraqi police but also from the United States Army's 173rd Airborne Brigade that had forcefully occupied the area to help protect American planes at Kirkuk Airbase.

Only a few weeks earlier, Mona had been hit by shrapnel in a night-time, hit-and-run firefight with a platoon of Marines. She had managed to knock down two or three of them before slipping away into the darkness. Someone threw a grenade that exploded close to her. A shard of metal hit her. It burned like fire, but she kept on her feet and managed to escape. The wound was a long tear in an inner thigh, and the sharp chunk of steel shrapnel had nicked an artery resulting in substantial blood loss.

Ironically, when Mona was injured, Fadia had managed to help her make her way to Camp Renegade, which was a well known American

medical treatment center in Iraq. Fadia left her
there with the enemy knowing full well that she
would be well cared for. She then spent several
days being patiently treated by American
military doctors working at the facility. She told
them she was a school teacher—an innocent
civilian and was hurt on her way to school when
someone detonated a roadside bomb, killing
several of her friends.

The doctors believed her story. She told it
with such passion, and she seemed so honest.
They were sympathetic toward Iraqi civilians
who were targeted by terrorists, and they bent
over backwards to help, especially women and
children. As soon as she could, Mona had
returned to the fighting, but it had been too
soon. The leg became infected and she had
traveled to Damascus for additional care when
the call for this mission came to her. Mona's
wound was still healing slowly, and her leg
constantly ached. The site of the wound, with
its long string of stitches, was an angry-color of
red, swollen, and quite sore to the touch.

While she was at Camp Renegade, Mona
had managed to secure quite a bit of useful
intelligence about the camp that she passed
along to other terrorists. That information
would eventually cost the lives of several of
the very people who had worked to save her
life. Their bad luck, she thought. She hated
Americans, and she especially despised those
who occupied Iraq. Death to America!

The fact was that both women could not

only handle any kind of automatic weapon, but they could also deal effectively with the men they fought along side of...and against. Fadia had accumulated considerable knowledge about explosives and was particularly skilled at the construction of the infamous and most deadly "roadside bombs" that had been so successful in killing and maiming literally thousands of Iranians and Americans. Most importantly, Fadia had been trained in how to activate explosive devices, and those she and Mona carried in their bags could be detonated easily. And, she knew the kind of damage the devices could do. She spent countless hours teaching Mona what she knew about explosives and, during the past few days, how to use the special ones contained in the wooden suitcases.

Like their male comrades, they both looked forward to the chance to become martyrs for the Jihad and Allah in the United States. They were excited about the possibility of this happening on the arrogant president's Texan soil. They both just wanted to be sure they did their parts to accomplish the mission. They were willing to give all they had, especially their lives, to this project.

CHAPTER FOUR

Hot Metal

YOU KNOW, I had made my mind up this wouldn't happen again," Molly said. "I don't want you to think there is any future in this, ever," she said roughly, as she pulled her boots on. "I keep telling you that, but somehow you keep me coming back...I don't know why I do it. I don't understand what hold you have over me. I don't even like you...there just flat out isn't any future in this, so you'd better get that through your thick Cajun head!" She stood up and stomped quickly down the narrow hallway to the front door.

Molly had to slam the door of the ancient mobile home several times to get it to latch. It kept popping back open every time she tried to close it. She finally gave it a mighty kick with the toe of her boot, denting the aluminum. It latched with a dull clicking sound. "Should have left the damned thing open," she said to herself. The metal skin of the mobile home was hot. As she stepped outside the back door, Molly burnt her hand slightly on the shiny metal siding and she steadied herself going down the steps. She'd drunk way too much the nite before, and had slept way too little.

"Dammit!," her voice cracked, as she jerked her hand away from the heat. "Gets me every time!" She strode with more than feigned angry determination toward her Jeep. As she walked, she turned her head slightly to look back to see if Owen was watching. As she squinted her eyes tightly to shield them from the intense sunlight, she could see the heat waves in shimmering lines rising from the roof of the mobile home, blurring the light blue of the sky in an odd way that only West Texans can truly understand. The rusty little air conditioning unit near the front door steps snapped, thumped, and rattled like a trail of tin cans behind a car as the compressor kicked in. Molly wondered to herself about why it was still running. She turned her head back toward the trailer and shouted, "That damned thing is going to quit you any time, Owen, just like me!" She hoped he was listening. More so, she secretly hoped he was watching her. Owen is good at keeping things going that should have played out long ago, sort of like our relationship, she thought.

Owen raised his head from a wad of sheets that had somehow become his pillow, at the sound of Molly's voice outside. He wondered what all the noise was about. He stirred and got up to look out the bedroom window just in time to see Molly's dirty green Wrangler heading out the driveway at full speed, with its big, nearly bald tires spitting gravel back toward the trailer, filling the air with a cloud of dust.

He glanced at the clock on his dresser and knew he was going to be late. He also noticed Molly's silver and turquoise earrings were next to his watch. Her favorites...guess I'd better get them back to her tonight before she thinks she's lost them...and, why the hell was she so damned upset? he thought. Owen remembered buying those earrings for her the last time he was in Albuquerque. They were Zuni, signed on the back. Molly loved them and wore them whenever she knew she would be seeing Owen.

Owen knew Preacher would suspect something this morning, since Owen was almost always on time. He worked at being punctual to a fault, especially at arriving at the operations building in the mornings. He wanted to be a good example for the Carps. The good thing was that Owen knew Preacher well enough to know he'd keep his mouth shut about this. That was the good thing about Preacher. He'd been there and done that with his own checkered past. He and Owen were considerably closer than the rest of the Carps. They had a mutual respect and trust that came from the knowledge of responsibility. Preacher had been the foreman for nearly twenty-five years before Owen took over. He wanted to "come down from the mountain," as he liked to say, so he gave up the job. He supported Owen from the very beginning, and single-handedly put out a few little fires that sometimes flare up to scorch new leadership.

Owen dressed hurriedly, headed out of the trailer and had the same trouble getting the door to latch that Molly did. He finally kicked the door shut, widening the dent that was already there. He jumped in his truck and raced himself to work, taking more than a few risks in making up time. Finally, Owen pulled in to the dusty lot in front of the main Carpenter operations building. He could see Preacher waiting impatiently at the door. He wondered how the morning's conversation would begin.

As expected, as soon as Owen stepped into the building, Preacher spoke up, saying "I was worried about you, Owen. You're never late. You didn't have any trouble did ya?" Preacher smiled at the uncomfortable look that Owen had all over his face. It was a look that told him the tale. Owen didn't say anything. The moments passed, each man waiting for the other to break the silence.

To Owen's relief, Preach spoke up, mercifully changing the subject to the day's work ahead by saying, "Hey, Pard, we need to get out and check the choke tubes and baffle plates in the Number Twelve reciprocating compressor unit. I just have a feeling we're going to have a problem there if we don't deal with it right away. Can't tell ya why...just a feeling. You know my feelings are usually right, Owen. There's a bit too much vibration coming out of that unit. I can hear it and what's more, I can feel trouble in my bones." Preacher continued to smile.

Owen walked past Preacher and sat down at his desk to look at his day's workplan before deciding when to commit time to dealing with the compressor unit that Preacher was worried about. Cowpaddy, Dinner-Roll, and Buster were already out in the fields. They'd gotten an early start since the heat index was going to be way high. Owen got on the two-way radio to check in with them. "Carpenter crew...what's your 10-20?"

Cowpaddy responded right away. Must be sitting in the truck...he responded way too quickly. He's taking the easy road already today. I'm going to have to give that boy a talking too very soon, he thought. Cowpaddy reported what Owen already knew. The crew was already working on a rotary-screw compressor unit at one of the more remote pumping stations. It was new technology. The rotary-screw replaced the reciprocating compressor. It was more efficient, but demanded a lot of tender loving care to keep running the way it was designed to run.

"College Boy is on it, Owen. He's got Buster on his hands and knees already...and you know how much he likes to do that do us," he joked. Owen was concerned. That unit had been down twice in the past few weeks and he didn't want it to go down again. Time was money. Owen said, "Well, git-er-done, Paddy. Fix it right this time, ok? Get out there and help them finish it up. We've got to take care of another problem at Number Twelve."

CHAPTER FIVE

Vera Cruz, Mexico

ERNARDO WAITED in the airport parking lot with Ashur, Said, and Samir. He was a genuinely friendly, large man, reaching just under six feet in height, and seriously overweight at nearly 300 pounds. He sweated, profusely, at the slightest exertion. Bernardo was the kind of man that could "procure" most anything. He had a talent for it. Bernardo was the designated contact for Damascan "enterprises" in Mexico. The cartel he worked for had been contracted by representatives of the alim. They had provided the cartel with a tidy sum of money to compensate for Bernardo's time and more than enough to quietly purchase very specific 'equipment and supplies.'

He had bought the old yellow Ford school bus for mere pesos. It had been parked for quite a while and wasn't running. It had a couple of flat tires. A large family of mice had moved in and taken over the foam in the driver's seat cushion. The rear of the bus was full of trash. Bernardo had worked the last couple of weeks evicting the mice, cleaning it up, and getting basic things fixed so that the bus was ready to travel. Well-used school buses from the States were in high demand throughout Mexico, and finding one that would take care of his new Syrian friends with some degree of dependability wasn't easy. But, Bernardo had done it. The fact was that anything could be done and anything could be bought for the right price in Mexico, including the fake ID's Bernardo had purchased for the group he was now to escort. He knew the pictures wouldn't match, but he had photos of two Mexican women and three Mexican men. He also knew that if they were stopped at the border, the American guards wouldn't notice anything but brown skin with what appeared to be proper papers. He even had a picture of himself made up to glue to the visor as the "driver."

The 1978 Ford "Bluebird" was originally used in some obscure little town in western Kansas, where it was driven into the ground hauling children to school, day after day, in all sorts of weather. The Unified School District markings still were visible beneath the side windows. The old V-8 motor smoked, the 2-speed didn't work any longer, and the clutch slipped a little. But, for some reason, it still ran fine. Lots of vehicles smoked in Mexico and no one paid the slightest bit of attention, unlike in the States where there would be a loud cry of moral and environmental outrage by the good citizens at the sight of their air being polluted. The old bus had been traded a couple of times over the years, and like so many other retired American school buses, eventually found its final destination to be south of the border. Bernardo had taken out most of the ragged seats and had painted the side windows to shield the interior from prying eyes. He'd just put in a new battery and added a couple of quarts of black bulk oil to the engine. Bernardo had built a large wooden storage box out of used plywood in the back of the bus. It was to be used for the weapons and ammunition. The storage was crudely built but looked like it belonged in the rattle-trap vehicle. Bernardo thought, The less suspicion accidentally drawn, the better. Finally, he felt the bus was ready to go anywhere.

It had been more difficult than he'd expected for Bernardo to fill the Syrian weapon's order. They had paid cash, up front, months ago. He had to find five fully automatic AK47 rifles, five semi-automatic Glock 9mm handguns, ammunition, four sticks of dynamite, and two dozen hand grenades. It wasn't like there weren't plenty of weapons in Mexico. Everyone had weapons. After all, Mexico was the land of revolution. Of late, the drug cartels had brought in thousands of automatic rifles. Cartel warfare and infighting was becoming more and more common. Shootings, bombings, and kidnappings had become a part of daily existence. Mexico was nearly in a state of anarchy, especially near the border with the United States. A lot of people with money were speculating, hanging on to guns expecting the market to go higher and higher. Mexico's President—and there was plenty of argument about who really was the President—had been ordering crackdowns on weapon possession and sales in the last couple of years. These days, only the bad guys or the wealthy had guns for sale in Mexico, and the guns were at a premium. Bernardo eventually had to ask the cartel for help in securing the weapons. The cartel came though almost overnight. It was that quick. Once again, the Syrians had provided so much cash for these kinds of eventualities that the cartel was only happy to oblige.

Ashur waited up in front on the bus with Bernardo resting quietly just behind the driver's seat. His cousins slept fitfully in the heat of the rear of the vehicle. They occasionally woke just long enough to brush nagging flies away from their sweating faces. Ashur and Bernardo were starting to become impatient as they waited and watched for new arrivals to Vera Cruz Airport—two special arrivals in particular. Those two would be easy to spot. There was no real terminal in Vera Cruz, just a very basic airport check in areas that held only a small number people. Most arriving passengers got off their planes, picked up their luggage, and made it quickly past the gates to catch transportation into town or off to their favorite seacoast resort. A long column of brightly colored taxis was lined up in front of the main check-in area, honking at one another, shouting expletives in Spanish, and maneuvering to pick up the next precious passenger. It was a situation of "every taxi driver for himself," and a very tough business.

In the parking lot across the street, where the bus was parked, a small pack of rats scampered back and forth from the sewage drain onto the hot, broken, trash-cluttered blacktop, looking for remnants of food people had pitched out of cars and buses. Meanwhile, large birds dived on the rats every now and then tying to catch an easy meal. Watching from the side, Ashur thought to himself, The rule of the desert persists, even here. Survival of the fittest.

Ashur stared out the rock-pecked windshield of the bus, his sandaled feet perched up on the rusted chrome rail in the entry step way. Bernardo's old jam box radio played Mexican tunes, one after another, with a mindless, chattering DJ breaking in between each song with nothing much to say. Flies buzzed in and out of the windows of the bus. Sweat dripped from his chin onto the front of his damp t-shirt. Ashur's mind drifted as he wondered to himself if he'd done the right thing so many years ago by asking those men for financial assistance to go to the United States for "education." He recalled being embarrassed, since his family had once been quite wealthy. The alim and his people seemed so pleased to send him. Ashur knew that one day there would be a price to pay on the debt, but the payback had come too soon for his liking. He wondered if he should have just stayed in Austin. Why had he left? He thought, "Lisa is there. I wonder if I will ever see her again? I wonder if she misses me like I miss her. I wonder if she'll survive what we are about to do?"

He wasn't willing to bet he'd see her again. He felt strongly that this was a one-way trip, and he was struggling to accept it as just that. He sensed finality. His life had been a short journey. Yet, Ashur wanted to see Lisa one last time. He worried that she'd suffer soon, and that he would be the cause. He didn't want to think about it.

Finally, there they were. Ashur spotted them right away. "Samir, Said—wake up! They're here," he shouted, almost too excitedly. Mona and Fadia walked directly from the airplane through a rusted steel gate in the fence leading from the airfield toward the taxi stands and parking lot area. Ashur thought, Anyone can get into Mexico . . . I hope Texas is this easy!

He got off the bus and trotted across the blacktop. His sandals made an annoying flopping sound as he ran, so he deliberately cut his stride back to silence them, as if it mattered with all the noise in the airport. He caught the women's attention between two taxis that were maneuvering to gain their business. They waved, and crossed the narrow street to the parking lot.

Ashur greeted them with the standard

Arabic hello, "Salaam, alaykum." The women, visibly shocked, glanced quickly at one another. Fadia looked around to make sure that no strangers were near. She walked up closely to Ashur and leaned into his ear.

She said, "You fool, speak English or Spanish...get used to it beginning now. Never use Arabic! We may soon need to be convincing that we belong in America or Mexico, and you never know who is listening!" Ashur was embarrassed. He knew he had made a mistake, and he sensed the women were already disappointed with him.

As they turned toward the bus, it was with some degree of relief, mixed with some secret level of angst that he noticed they had arrived with the baggage he'd been expecting. After all, the entire mission would have had to be cancelled had they lost the bombs. The trio walked over to the sweltering, faded yellow, bus and boarded. Fadia and Mona gave their special baggage to Said who had come to the front of the bus to greet them. He took their bags and carefully returned to the rear. He sat them down on the rubber aisle floor and opened them as if her were opening a carton of eggs. He removed the small wooden boxes and stowed them in a rather large plastic storage container. He placed foam packing in between each suitcase. He carefully packed them, making sure they were cushioned all the way around.

"No sense blowing ourselves up yet," he said quietly to Samir who watched him lazily from a Spartan metal/cushioned bunk that had been fashioned from old bus seat parts across the aisle. "Yes, there is enough explosive power here to turn us and this airport to vapor, Samir. What would the alim say back in Damascus if we had an accident and really blew ourselves up? Poor bastards...but they were too stupid to carry out the plans...we should have sent another team..." Samir's thoughts traveled to a vision he often had of their parents' home in Damascus. He could almost smell his mother's cooking. He hadn't had a good meal in months. He realized he was very, very hungry.

Both he and Said had spent time in Afghanistan, and then later in Iran. Like the women, they were battle-hardened, and they had been prepared from birth to be martyrs for the cause at the asking. It was their long, mutually beneficial, connections with opium dealers in Afghanistan that had proven to be so valuable in putting the plan together. The two brothers had both been narco-terrorists, funded in full by joint al-Quaeda and Talliban organizations. Just a small part of the annual production of 360 tons of morphine and heroin generated enough cash to finance multiple terrorist programs throughout the middle east, and, in fact, anywhere in the world. A promise had been made to the Cali, a Mexican drug gang with connections to border groups who muled through the border town of Presidio in Texas. In return for that promise, Bernardo had purchased, with Syrian supplied money, not only the bus, the fake ID's, but also the rifles, handguns, and supplies – enough to get the group to the border with Texas at Presidio.

Bernardo had worked with two different cartels in his brief, young career. This cartel was quite dangerous. The principals had no respect for the old ways. They didn't play the game with the power structure. They rode roughshod over anyone unfortunate enough to get in their way. Bernardo often wondered how long his life would be spared if he made the slightest mistake. On this assignment, his directions had been simple and clear. Get the bus. Buy the equipment. Drive the team to the border. They could try driving through first. He'd driven through many times without being stopped. If they were stopped, they had the ID's. If this didn't work, he would show them the not-so-secret foot bridge. That was the plan. It was so simple.

Bernardo remembered telling the boss, "I can do this with my eyes closed!" A native of Vera Cruz, Bernardo had made many trips to Presidio and had crossed the foot bridge several times into Texas without any problems at all. He knew the route that was for sure. He knew how to bribe police. And he knew his job. He was determined to prove his worth to the cartel. He did wonder what was in the wooden boxes that seemed to be so valuable to the Syrians. But, he didn't ask. He knew better than to know too much. But...he wondered.

CHAPTER SIX

The Mudlogger

MUDLOGGERS are highly educated and well trained oil and gas field geologists. They are usually contract people who work for service companies that support drilling teams. They record the speed of the drillings, clean and dry drilling samples; record the lithology—the nature of the mineral content— of a well. They constantly collect, process, and log geological samples from well sites, and they provide invaluable information to the drillers that can make or break the success of a drilling team. A good mudlogger can, from accurate analysis of the data they accumulate, predict dangerous situations, such as over-pressured formations that might wind up blowing the hell out of a team during coring operations. They are essential personnel for successful oil and gas field crews. Owen had the best mudlogger in west Texas. She was worth her weight in oil.

Candy was a "big ole girl." At 5'10", and 275 pounds, she could hold her own with any roughneck in pretty much any situation. And she had more than her share of attitude. She could be as tough and as gritty as any of them, and she could cuss and drink most of them under the table. On a bet, Candy had beaten the entire crew, one at a time, at arm wrestling one raucous nite at the Social Club. Well, she had beaten everyone except Dinner Roll, and he held the dubious honor of beating her after a horrific struggle.

The truth of it was that Candy didn't have to work. Her father had owned half of Pecos County and made a fortune buying and selling mineral rights. She was an only child. Her mother had died giving birth to her, and she'd grown up under her father's watchful eye in the oil and gas fields. She had left West Texas only for a few short years to study geological engineering at the University of Missouri in Rolla. Candy's father had passed away a few years back and left close to twenty million dollars, as well as 40 sections of land near Pecos, to Candy. When she got the contract to work for Carpenter, she'd paid cash for a section of land just north of Crane so she could be close to the fields that Carpenter's crews worked. She moved in a modular home, put up a huge metal building, and fenced the property all in a month's time.

"It's amazing what money can do," she boasted whenever she drank too much. Candy liked the country, and she liked horses, too. She had several, and she had a couple of big dogs...and she had anything else she wanted—

that is, except for one thing, and she wasn't about to give up trying to get it.

It was pretty evident that Candy worked because she liked being around the men, and one man in particular. Preacher. It didn't matter to her that he was more than twice her age, or that she was twice his size. She wanted him in the worst way. He was so much like her father. He even resembled her father, she'd thought. She knew about his wayward past, but it didn't matter to her. She knew he liked to run the women, but she was certain she could take that out of him. Her motto, when it came to Preacher, was any time, any place, and she wasn't just talking. Owen had walked up on the two of them, more than once, going at it like rabbits in the front seat of Preacher's old Ford truck in the noisy shade of a drilling unit.

Candy had offered him a lifetime of never having to work again if he'd just marry her, and she'd made the offer more than once. The fact was that she made the offer almost every day. She gave him expensive gifts that he didn't need. She bought him clothes, watches, hats. She'd been recently trying to talk him into driving her new yellow Hummer. She said if he wanted it, it was his. Preacher liked his old Ford, though, and teased her he'd be embarrassed to drive something that looked like a school bus. She would track Preacher down in the fields, bring him a cold drink...a sandwich, and maybe some homemade cake.

They'd been seeing each other, on and

off—mostly on --for over a year. Preacher kept holding out. Candy would get him all liquored up and push him as hard as she could, but he still held out. Owen often wondered how Preacher reconciled his "sinful" ways with his conscience, but he hadn't ever said a word to him about it. Owen didn't much like Candy, mostly because he figured she'd eventually take Preacher away from his crew. After all, he needed Preacher to keep things running...but mostly, he needed his friendship.

CHAPTER SEVEN

The Crossing

ADAY'S DRIVE was all it took. Ashur couldn't believe it. He was amazed that they'd made their way up the Mexican blacktop to Presidio in a single day. The stretch looked so big on the map. It was evening and the sun was beginning to set. The only stops they'd made were at two gasoline stations. The old bus had done its job well, and Bernardo knew the route. No one had bothered to check them at all. It was surreal. They just drove north all the way to the border.

Ojinaga, locally known as "OJ," was a dirty little Rio Grande border town. Ashur was a bit naïve about this part of the country and had expected better, with its proximity to the United States. After all, Texas, around Austin, was quite nice. He didn't think it was all that far away, but it was. The roadside along the highway was lined with run-down businesses, restaurants, and night clubs that appeared to be closed but probably weren't. And there were people walking, lots of people walking in the direction of the border crossing. Some carried small bags, others carried nothing. The walkers shared a look of exhaustion. Oddly, chickens were everywhere. Ashur wondered about that. Why so many chickens? The housing that could be seen from the road was incredibly run down. It appeared that people lived in shacks. Many of the houses had broken out windows and doorways that stood open. Garbage and trash littered the streets. It was so much worse than the mostly hidden slum areas in Austin, Ashur thought, and certainly worse than anywhere in Syria.

The highway through OJ either headed south or north. The first town to the north was Presidio, Texas. Few cars were traveling south, and literally no foot traffic headed that way. There would be Federales at the border on the south side and the US Border Patrol on the north. Spending too much time on either side would be risky. There was a foot bridge a mile or two south, and it went largely unguarded on either side. The problem was that using it would mean abandoning the bus and finding new transportation in Texas. Ashur had to decide. What was the least risk? There was so much at stake here. They couldn't afford to lose the bombs and that was a certainty. If they lost them, they could never go home again. In fact, if they were caught with them, they'd likely wind up in the Supermax Security Prison in Denver for the rest of their lives. Either way, martyrdom would be denied to them.

Ashur had talked at length with Bernardo on the drive up the highway from Vera Cruz. They had discussed the pros and cons of trying to drive through the border or walking across. If they walked across, they would have to either buy, or steal a large enough vehicle to get them another five or six hours deeper into Texas. It would take time to locate the vehicle, and time would provide too much opportunity to draw suspicion. There was so much risk Ashur had been debating this for hours, and the time had come to decide what to do. He was the leader of the group and the responsibility fell to him alone.

"Bernardo, drive through the border. Samir and Said, sit next to Mona and Fadia. If you are asked, you are visiting family and show your ID's. Put your handguns under your clothing, but keep them close at hand. If we are pressed, be prepared to shoot."

Bernardo pulled the bus into the "nothing to declare" lane. The light was red. They stopped and waited. They held their breath and watched for any sign that they were going to be inspected. It was dead quiet on the bus. The only sound was the rumbling of the idling old Ford engine. The rank exhaust of the bus seeped into the open side windows and the air was sickening. They could hear talking outside as the guards talked to drivers in the "declaration" lane. One car, with what appeared to be a white American driver, was pulled to the side with its trunk open. There were Mexican

Police with guns rummaging through baggage in the trunk. Other guards stood at the crossing station itself, but curiously, none even glanced at the bus. The green light, signaling pass was lit, so Bernardo simply drove slowly across the border. The guards on the Texas side didn't even glance their way and waved them through.

They were stunned. Who would have believed that a busload of armed Syrians could cross the border into Texas, with guns and bombs, totally unchecked? It made no sense to Ashur. Anyone could have done it! They all stared at each other with looks of shock and disbelief, but they were relieved. The major obstacle to moving the bombs to Texas had been handled with ease. They were in Presidio, Texas – armed and deadly – and no one had the slightest clue.

Bernardo headed up US Highway 67 to the north toward Pecos County. He thought they could be in the middle of the oil and gas fields by early morning. The old school bus rattled along, bouncing with every bump and leaving behind it a trail of blue smoke.

Eventually, they had to stop for fuel and came upon an isolated little convenience store. An old Buick sedan sat along side the store. The place was practically deserted. It was run by an older woman and her husband. She ran the cash register while he moved around the store in a wheel chair stocking shelves and keeping the place in order. The group took turns using the facilities while Bernardo stood along side and filled up the tanks on the bus. The wind had picked up and dust was blowing across the parking lot. Bernardo covered his eyes with his hands while the pump ran.

The woman inside watched the group intently. She could tell that they weren't local and she wondered aloud to her husband what a school bus from Kansas was doing in Texas.

"What are they up to? Something doesn't feel right about them. They don't look quite right. Come here and take a look," she said out loud. Her husband either didn't hear her or he ignored her as he busily worked at reorganizing a lower shelf of mostly outdated canned goods.

Eventually, Bernardo came in to pay for the fuel. The woman took his money and as she was counting out the change, said "You folks from around here?"

Bernardo said, "We've been taking a little trip." He stumbled and quickly added, "We're from Dallas." The woman glanced outside, watching Mona and Fadia climbing back on the bus. Bernardo gathered up the change and hurried out the door.

She murmured, Uh huh, right, mostly to herself. But Bernardo heard her.

She turned to her husband and said, "Are you listening to me! There's something funny about them. Maybe we should...." she stopped mid sentence.

As he boarded the bus, Bernardo said, with a voice that sounded alarmed, "They are a little too curious. We need to get on out of here."

At that, Mona stood up and said, "Wait. I won't be long." She walked silently past Ashur without even glancing at him, stepped off the bus, and went back into the convenience store. She reached under her coat and pulled out her Glock. She pointed it at the terrified woman's head, and moved close to her... pointed the gun at her forehead and pulled the trigger. As she turned to leave, the old man began screaming for help. And, of course, there was no help. In fact, no one would come into the store until the next day as it was closing time. Mona walked back to him and coolly fired a single round into his face. She didn't flinch. The old man slumped over in his wheel chair, at the same time dropping a jar of Bush's Chili to the floor. The jar shattered. Mona put the gun away and walked calmly to the doorway, shut off the lights to the store, and went outside to re-board the bus. As she climbed the steps, she looked at Bernardo, who by now had the bus running, and said "Let's go." No one spoke. Ashur felt ashamed for not having done what he knew Mona had done. He sat silently, looking straight ahead.

The bus lumbered out of the gravel parking lot and back onto the blacktop. It wasn't long before they noticed the intensity of the wind. The group couldn't believe how strong it had suddenly become, blowing them along from behind.

"At least it is a tailwind," Bernardo said aloud. "We'll save a lot of gasoline! But this blowing sand and dirt...it reminds me of home! You might raise the windows as far as you can stand it. Otherwise we are going to have a lot of dirt in here before long."

CHAPTER EIGHT

The Social Club

IT WAS NEARLY 10:00 PM before the crew made it to the Social Club. It had been a scorcher of a day, and when the wind picked up in the late afternoon, the dust became problematic at one of the drilling sites. College Boy had torn down a pumping unit to replace a solenoid that had been acting up. Before he could get it back together, the equipment had begun filling with the blowing red dirt from the desert. He tried to put a temporary tarp over it, but the wind grabbed the tarp like paper and pitched it high into the air. College Boy got on the two-way and called for help. In just a few minutes, Owen, Buster, and Dinner Roll pulled in. They slid the company's lumbering Dodge crew cab to a stop and rushed over to help get the equipment secured.

Three hours later, they had it done, but the wind and dust had worsened to the point that seeing the road out was an issue. Owen led the way out, with College Boy right behind him in his new red Pontiac. Owen thought, This is no country for a 400 HP GTO. What the hell is he thinking?

The going was slow. Owen knew there were two cattle guards somewhere on the road ahead. He crawled the Dodge along. Dirt and dust were seeping in from the doors and the air was getting pretty thick with them. Finally, he came to the first cattle guard and clattered across it. Not far down the road was the second one.

Buster complained, "Dammit, I hate this country!" Dinner Roll took offense, and snapped "If you don't like it, move! It is always windy and dirty here. Don't you get it?" Buster tensed, and Owen quickly intervened. "All right you idiots. Give it a rest. We'll be damned lucky to get to the Social Club without running into something."

They hit the highway with a thud from the edge of the gravel road. Owen spun the Dodge down the road with College Boy passing him. Owen cursed at him as he flew by them, "Damn you, Garber!" The crew knew that when Owen dropped the nicknames, he was pissed. It didn't happen often, but when it did, they paid attention. It was likely that College Boy knew he was pushing the limit a bit.

The crew met at the Social Club every Friday nite. This was no exception. They were hungry and thirsty. They saw the neon beer signs lit up like Christmas when they turned into the parking lot. Owen pulled up to the rails in front of the Club. Preacher's old Ford truck and Paddy's Toyota truck, were sitting there next to a red Pontiac. There were several other familiar vehicles there that belonged to locals. One thing for sure, Owen thought to himself, College Boy was going to have a little talkin' to a bit later.

The trio jumped out of the Dodge and headed up the creaky steps. They could hear the familiar country western music as they swung the screen door open and pushed the heavy wooden door aside to walk in. Owen forced the door closed as quickly as he could, fighting the wind that was slamming into it head-on from the south. The screen door smacked against the outside wall of the building and broke off the hinges.

"Jesus," Owen shouted. "What the hell is up with this damned wind? It is supposed to slow down, isn't it?"

The place was busy. It was Friday night, after all, and there was nowhere else to go within an hour or more. Fort Stockton was probably the closest place, but no one wanted the drive home after taking on a load, late at nite, especially in a raging dust storm. The special was Molly's pot roast. No one made pot roast quite as good as Molly. She had the touch. She made it up in several large crock pots that seemed to empty out all too soon.

Fortunately for the three Carps, there was plenty left. Molly had baked biscuits too.

Preach and Paddy were already finished eating and were on their third or fourth—or maybe fifth— long neck. Preach was up dancing with one of the local girls. Paddy was shooting pool on the Club's sole table and talking loudly. It was the usual Friday evening at the Social Club. Owen reached behind the bar and grabbed three beers and they all sat at the bar. Molly served up the pot roast and biscuits.

"Want some honey?" she asked.

"Damned right!" said Buster, spitting bits of food as he inhaled it. He was trying to talk and eat at the same time. A day's hard work in the oil fields makes a man hungry beyond words, and common table manners become non-existent.

The boys at the bar turned to look when headlights suddenly flooded into the front windows of the Club. They could tell from the size of the vehicle that pulled in who it likely was. Momentarily, the heavy wooden front door flew open. It was the mudlogger. She immediately spotted Preacher, slow-dancing in the middle of the tiny dance floor with one of his female admirers.

She strode over to them, tapped her on the shoulder, roughly shoved her away and said "Private property, Bitch!" There was no dispute. The lady retreated without complaint. Preacher grabbed Candy up in his arms, at least as much as he could, and acted like he'd been dancing with her all evening.

"They are an odd couple," Owen said to

himself. "An unlikely couple." He could tell she was talking at him, a mile a minute. "No telling what she's laying on him now. Poor guy!" Owen almost felt sorry for Preacher, except he knew he could take care of himself.

Molly looked good tonight. She knew it. She did it for Owen, but she'd never admit it. Her hair was pulled back in a pony tail. She wore a tight tee-shirt and a pair of faded blue jeans that showed her perfect figure...perfectly. She leaned over the bar to be close for a bit to Owen, as she set the second longneck beer in front on him. Molly noticed the moment he walked in that he hadn't shaved today. He had just the right amount of growth to show the outline of what she saw as his wonderful dark beard. He's the sexiest man alive! she thought. She loved, but feared to some extent, his piercing blue eyes. Her fear was that she'd fall deeply in love with him, and he'd walk away. However, he definitely had the look. She didn't say a word. She just watched him silently as he enjoyed her pot roast and washed it down with long draughts of cold Budweiser.

Owen spun around in his stool and surveyed the bar room. Besides his crew, he recognized practically everyone, except the older, distinguished looking gentleman and a younger woman who sat closely on one of the Club's old school bus seats in front of the wooden spool that served as their table. They talked quietly. Probably passing through, he thought. Wonder how they knew to stop here?

He looks like a lawyer or a judge. Just the type, but it doesn't matter. Who cares?

Preacher had been watching the boys put the beer away, with raised eyebrows. He didn't approve, not that he hadn't been doing the same thing. Owen thought, He's such a contradiction...a damned hypocrite. It was one of those do-as-I say, not as- I-do things with Preacher sometimes, like now.

He and Candy finally walked over to get another beer from the bar. Preacher got close to Owen's ear and said something about "a flood upon the world of the ungodly." Owen wasn't in the mood. He leaned back and asked Candy, "How y'all doin' tonite?" Candy held Preacher close to her side and gave him a squeeze that might have broken a lesser man's back, and said "We are going to have quite a night – right, Preach?" She winked at Owen. He suspected he knew what interested Preach so much about Candy, and it wasn't her money.

CHAPTER NINE

Sand and Dirt

THE OLD FORD'S motor shuddered. It was becoming harder and harder to keep it running, let alone on the blacktop. The carburetor was probably taking in more than just air, jamming the fuel lines. The wind was intense and unrelenting. It blew sand and dirt into every possible crevice in the bus and the air inside was clouded and rank. Bernardo fought to hold the steering wheel steady. It had enough slack in it from its many years of hard service already, and the wind simply made matters worse. The sun was setting and visibility was decreasing rapidly. Bernardo worried he'd run into the back of a stalled vehicle, and with the "packages" on board, he knew the bus would likely blow sky high if that happened. He wasn't ready to die.

Ashur stumbled to the front of the swaying bus. He sat down behind Bernardo and tried to watch the road ahead. He could tell Bernardo was growing tired and impatient from battling the bus.

"Hey, we don't have that much farther to do. It's all good. Take it easy...we'll make it."

Bernardo replied, "I thought this bus was in better condition...I'm sorry it is having so much trouble! Can you look at the map and tell me how much farther we have before we get there?"

Ashur pulled out a soiled and well-used map of Texas. He was guessing when he said, "Maybe another 40 miles or so." Bernardo nodded that he understood, as he wrestled with the steering wheel. "I hope I can keep this thing running another hour or two. It's getting more and more difficult. I think it has sand in the fuel. And, we need to fill it up again with gasoline at the next place we come to. I want to be sure we can get back to the border."

"We drive in these conditions constantly in Syria, Bernardo," Ashur retorted. "This is just a light dusting, "he mused. "We'll make it."

Ashur wondered if there was any need to even consider a return trip with the bus. The little group had talked much of the way up into Texas from Vera Cruz. The conversation had deliberately avoided what they'd do...afterwards. Ashur thought that it was almost as if they were all resigned to the fact that this was a one-way mission. It was clear they were all ready to give their lives for Allah and the Jihad. And, the incredible significance of what they were about to do would give them all guaranteed immortality in the memories of their friends, family, and countrymen.

But still, Ashur worried. The rhetoric was fine, but in the innermost recesses of his mind, he worried if he had the nerve to set off those devices and never see Lisa, or anything he loved, ever again. Maybe he'd spent too much time in the United States. Maybe he had given up something of himself.

CHAPTER TEN

Camp Renegade, Iraq

THE U.S. Military intelligence headquarters in Iraq could not believe what happened. Insurgents had carried off a precision attack on one of the country's most important American military hospitals. Mortar rounds had fallen on the very spot in the camp that the doctors and nursing personnel thought was the most secure. How would anyone have known where to hit them? Surely no one who had been treated in the facility would give the information to the insurgents. Why would they? The military had spent months disguising the area to look nondescript. And, now, mortars landed there as if they had been perfectly guided. Someone had paid attention and provided flawless intelligence to the enemy. There was no other explanation.

No one knew for sure, but estimates were that a dozen rounds landed on the assembly area for the morning's briefing. Most of the camp's senior medical officers, including eight doctors and eleven nurses, had been killed instantly. Several others were wounded seriously. The camp would be essentially out of business for weeks until new personnel could be gathered up and flown in as replacements. Even then, it would take longer for the new people to get into a routine.

Camp Renegade was in chaos, but that was what somebody somewhere clearly intended.

CHAPTER ELEVEN

Taking the Ditch

BERNARDO had nursed the bus along in the dust storm within a mile or two of Girvin, but it was very slow going. He just couldn't see far ahead. The two-lane blacktop seemed to narrow in the darkness, and the visibility ahead wasn't more than a couple of dozen yards. Bernardo didn't spot the deer standing at the middle of the highway until it was too late. There were three of them, standing in a little tight group staring at the oncoming bus. He locked up the brakes on the old Ford and the bus slid sideways, crossing into the oncoming lane, missing the deer completely. Bernardo fought the steering wheel as the awkward bus reeled out of control off the blacktop and into the grader ditch along side the road. The side door slammed open. Bernardo instinctively reached for the pull bar, but the door was jammed and it caught the raised road shoulder just enough to rip it off with a loud bang!

As the bus slowed, it ran over countless large rocks and a road sign in the desert ditch. Finally, one of the rear dual tires blew. Bernardo managed to brake the bus, jerking it out of the ditch and into the desert, and finally got it stopped after running down a growth of mesquite beneath the lumbering vehicle. It had slid along for fifty or sixty yards into the desert before stopping. The engine was hot and the radiator was boiling over. Steam was venting from the sides and front of the huge faded yellow hood of the bus. It smelled hot, like burning rubber. Fumes and light gray smoke began filling the bus cabin, along with blowing dirt and sand that now found its way into the open doorway of the bus.

"The loose sand had likely kept the bus from rolling when it hit the ditch," Bernardo said outloud. "We were lucky."

The five passengers were stunned. Bernardo looked back down the aisle to see if anyone seemed hurt. It was deadly quiet for just a moment.

Mona was the first to speak. "We've got to get our equipment out of here. If there's a fire, it's over for us!" In a panic, the women grabbed the two suitcases, a bag with weapons, and pushed open the back emergency door of the bus. Mona jumped out and Fadia handed things to her as carefully as she could. Said and Samir picked up the remaining backpacks, the weapons, clips of ammo, and grenades and bailed out just behind Mona. Ashur walked toward the rear of the bus as Bernardo climbed out of the side door and helped Fadia finish unloading the equipment.

As Ashur and Fadia climbed out, Mona shouted, "Did you get it all? Listen to me...did you get it all?"

Ashur replied, "We have it all, Mona. Come on and let's get back away from the bus." Just as Ashur spoke, a more intense electrical fire began burning under the hood of the bus and darker smoke billowed through down the aisle and out the open rear doorway. The group gathered up a safe distance away in the darkness, out of easy sight from the highway. They stood in a circle along what seemed to be a gravel road that led someplace into the night, off of the blacktop.

"Must be a utility or well site service road of some kind. I don't see any lights." Ashur said.

"What do we do now?" asked Samir.

Said chimed in, "Yes, what now? We don't know where we are, do we? Maybe we need to turn back? How can we carry out our plan under these conditions?"

Mona said, "I won't hear this talk of going back! Stop it now, you spineless ass!" She had her Glock in her hand in an instant and it was clear that no one would be heading back until the mission was done.

Just then, Bernardo pointed up the highway, and between gusts of angry wind and blowing red dust, the lights of the Social Club dimly shown through the darkness. "Look. There's something over there, up the highway just a little further."

Fadia responded, "We need to avoid these Americans, no matter what. We have to keep the element of surprise or all will be lost. We don't have much time."

Just as Ashur was about to show a little embarrassed leadership and suggest a new plan, Bernardo shouted, "Look...someone is coming!" They dived for cover in the nearby mesquite just off the road and waited, hoping with futility that the smoldering bus would not be noticed.

CHAPTER TWELVE

The Hummer

A S CANDY AND PREACHER tried to sneak invisibly out the side door of the Social Club, Owen watched them out of the corner of his eye. They were locked arm in arm, each looking back to see if they'd been seen, heading quickly toward Candy's big yellow Hummer. College Boy spied them too, and went over to the doorway and shouted,

"Hey, where you two goin'... it's miserable out there!" They couldn't hear him, and as he and Owen watched, they jumped into the Hummer. The lights came on as the vehicle backed around and pulled out of the lot. There's something poetic about that truck being named Hummer, Owen thought to himself, and a huge smile lit up his tanned, rugged, face.

Molly noticed and said, "Owen... what are you so damned happy about? Did I miss something?"

Preacher steered Candy's rig out of the parking lot and down the blacktop. She was all over him, leaning heavily over the console, running her hand up and down his inner thigh and kissing his neck playfully. He could hardly concentrate on the road.

"You remind me of a high school kid, Candy! Slow down or this will be over before we have a chance to have any fun with it!" They were heading to their favorite, late night haunt. It wasn't far from the Social Club, just a mile or so. The old gas rig road had been the perfect meeting place to head to from the Club, when "something came up."

Preacher was going a bit slower than usual, with the wind and dust being so bad. He was about to turn up the gravel road when he saw a vehicle in the ditch. The engine fire was flickering just enough for him to notice.

"What the hell is that?" Candy said.

"Looks like a school bus with a fire on board, but what's it doing way out here this time of night, and a Friday at that!" replied Preacher as he wheeled the Hummer around and pulled in just ahead of the bus.

The Hummer's headlights lit up the front of the bus. Preacher reached down and flipped on the extra lights that were mounted on the Hummer's bumper. There was no movement on the bus, at least none that they could see. The windows were partially open and the side door seemed to be gone.

Preacher said, "Wait here, Candy." He jumped out and walked up to the bus. There was still no sign of life. He stepped up into the side doorway and tried to look in. The bus was filled with foul smelling smoke. He couldn't see a thing, and he shouted, "Anyone in here? Anyone hurt?" There was no response. Preacher turned and went back to the Hummer.

"You got a light of any kind, Candy?" She got out and opened the back door. She unsnapped a large plastic tool box and reached in to pull out a flashlight. Preacher took the light and went back to the bus.

He climbed on board and quickly walked down the aisle, shining the light back and forth. There was no one on board, for sure. He noticed candy bar wrappers, empty water bottles, what looked like bunks, and the crudely built-in storage in the back. He thought, This isn't a school bus. Someone's been traveling in it. Several someones, in fact, from the look of things.

He jumped off the bus from the edge of the aisle at the back emergency doorway and looked around outside, flashing the light into the mesquite. It was impossible to see very far, with the dust and darkness, but it was clear that there was no one nearby. He walked back to the Hummer and got in with Candy. The Hummer's engine was running and the AC felt cool as it sensed the door open and began blowing stronger in his face. Nothing like automatic climate control, he thought.

Candy said, "Preach, what's going on? Did you find anyone in there?"

Preacher said, "Strange. Very strange,

Candy. I don't know what to make of it. There's no one there. No sign of anyone, inside or out. It looks like they had an engine fire and pulled over. Odd we didn't pass them coming from the Social Club. Seems like they would have walked up there for help."

Suddenly, Candy's eyes grew large as she looked past Preacher out the side of the Hummer. Someone was standing there. She could just see a dark shape of a person very near the vehicle. As she pointed, she said, "Preach...look, there's someone there!"

Preacher turned too look. Just as he did, the side window exploded in hundreds of tiny pieces into his face. The pop-pop-pop firing of a handgun was muffled in the howling wind. Preacher's head suddenly blew apart in a spray of blood, hitting Candy in the eyes and showering her with small bits of the back of his skull, blood, and chunks of the window glass.

She screamed, "Preacher!" as she ducked down in his lap to avoid being shot. Pop-pop-pop the handgun spoke again, somehow missing Candy. She grabbed the shifter, pushed a hand down on the brake and crunched the transmission into drive. She reached over and shoved the foot throttle to the floor with her hand. The Hummer leaped forward, throwing sand and rocks in every direction as she ran over whatever was in the way of the lumbering SUV. The Hummer smacked up along side the bus, scraping its way down toward the rear of it. Candy dared not look up. She kept down and blindly pushed the Hummer into the brush quite a ways, pounding its way through mesquite and over the rocks.

Candy finally let the Hummer slow. She looked back and could see nothing. She took a chance and got out, running around the front of the vehicle and opening up the driver's door. She pulled Preacher's lifeless body out, opened the rear door, and pushed him into the back seat. She let his body settle as gently as she could into the soft leather. She slammed the door and climbed into the driver's seat. She drove the Hummer as hard as she could back toward the highway, jumping the grader ditch and bouncing onto the blacktop. She floorboarded the Hummer and screamed down the blacktop until she was sure she'd left the bus and the shooter far behind.

She was crying, shaking, confused. She glanced into the back and could see Preacher's lifeless form slumped along the back seat. She didn't want to accept the truth that her Preacher was gone forever. Maybe he'll be ok...maybe we can save him, she thought.

Candy was frantic. Her mind was whirling with one thought after another about what to do next. Suddenly, she realized she was heading away from the Social Club. She said out loud, "My God! We've got to get to the Club! What was I doing going the wrong way?" She braked the Hummer hard and spun it around in the middle of the blacktop. She stomped the gas peddled to the floor and charged back the way she had just come. I've got to get help for Preacher! Maybe he'll be all right. Maybe we can call for help there! she thought.

CHAPTER THIRTEEN

It Begins

AS THEY WATCHED the Hummer speed down the highway, Ashur shouted, "Mona! What were you thinking! Now they know we are here. Now they will be after us! We no longer have the element of surprise on our side. You should have let them go. There was no reason to have done that!"

Mona glared at Ashur, "You are a complete idiot! How do you think we will get anywhere without a vehicle?" That was our ticket to our destination! We needed that vehicle!" she screamed.

Ashur turned to the group, all but Mona were standing behind him. He said, "People, we are at our destination. It happens here. It happens now. The map has shown us that for the last hour or so that we've been in the Permian Basin. There are oil and gas wells everywhere here. We are in the middle of it all!

See that sign?" He pointed to a metal sign next to the gravel road. It read, CARPENTER GAS ACCESS ROAD – NO TRESPASSING.

"This road leads to a well or pipeline site. There's one just like this on the other side of the highway. I saw the sign when we were by the bus."

Said and Samir whispered to one another. It was clear they were shaken. So much had happened in such a short time to threaten the entire mission. Even though all of them but Ashur and Bernardo were combat veterans, they still feared failure. The greatest fear was dying in the desert for nothing. There'd be no glory or praise in that kind of useless death. They had to finish the mission ... the Jihad had to be carried out.

Fadia said, "We will do this. Gather your strength. Think! We have to get moving before they come after us."

Ashur replied, "She's right. Bernardo, divide up the weapons. We must go now or risk being caught. They won't have any idea why we are here or what direction we went, especially in this weather along with the darkness. Mona, Fadia ... you've handled the bombs this far, it remains your task to carry them to their destinations. This won't be hard. Let's set them off a few miles apart. Said and Samir, you go with Mona. Bernardo and I will go with Fadia to the other side of the highway. We will set the timers to explode the devices precisely at 2:00 AM."

Bernardo looked up with a start. He said, "Wait! My job was to get you here, not to help. I have no skills! You don't need me for this. I can go back and work on the bus...."

Ashur stared coldly at Bernardo and said, "You have a choice, my friend. Stay here, dead, or help. You decide." As he spoke, Ashur pulled out his 9mm and pointed it at Bernardo. He didn't know if he could use the gun or not, but he knew he had to show his strength now, or never.

"You misunderstand me! I'll help. Just tell me what you want me to do." said, Bernardo.

Ashur lowered his weapon and said, "A wise decision. We need you to help us escape. You know this country. But right now, we need you to help us with the devices. We won't need the bus. It can't be fixed and you know it. We will need you to help us get another vehicle and drive us out of here. You can work on the bus when we are ready to leave."

Ashur turned to the group, "Be sure and keep your bearings. As soon as the devices are set to explode, head to the highway. We will meet by the bus. Set your walkie-talkies on channel 6. The two groups kneeled and prayed silently. Then, they rose and the two groups headed off in opposite directions.

CHAPTER FOURTEEN

Alarm!

CANDY SKIDDED the Hummer into the parking lot and almost up to the door of the Social Club. She reached behind her and grabbed Preacher's wrist to check to see if he had a pulse, knowing already that there would be none. His arm felt cold. She knew he was stone dead, but she hoped it wasn't too late. She opened her door and jumped out, catching her foot on the side rail, falling into the gravel lot.

"Dammit!" she screamed, as she tumbled to the ground, skinning the palms of her hands in the rough gravel. "Dammit! Help!" The music was blaring inside the Club. No one could hear. She stumbled up to the door and flung it wide open. Everyone in the Club turned and looked with shock at Candy's blood-soaked face.

She screamed, "My God! We thought a school bus had crashed and stopped to help. Then, someone killed Preacher! Back down by the gas rig dirt road. They just walked up to the window and shot him. He didn't have a chance! You've got to help him!"

She broke down, sobbing. The place was momentarily silent, as the words sank in. Then they began moving toward her. Owen jumped off the barstool. Molly came around the bar and the pair ran over to Candy. She slumped to her knees and completely collapsed on the floor. She was splattered with blood, glass, and bits of Preacher's skull and brains. Owen knew this was all too real.

"Molly, see if you can calm her down. Do whatever you need to do to help her, ok?" Owen ran outside to the Hummer. The others knew instinctively not to follow. They stood at the windows of the Girvin Social Club, looking out into the darkness at the Hummer. Preacher was Owen's friend.

As he ran up to the vehicle, Owen could immediately see that the window glass on the driver's side was gone. He pulled open the front door and looked inside the Hummer. There was shattered glass and blood everywhere. He could see Preacher was in the back seat. He opened the rear door and saw Preacher lying there, quietly. His friend was gone. Owen felt his stomach turn, and his eyes glazed with tears. He was close to Preach, at least as close as men become who go through trials and tribulations together. They had a special bond. He was one of the few men Owen had ever trusted.

Owen stepped up into the Hummer and

reached gently under Preacher's arms and back and pulled him up to take him inside. Preacher's head rolled to the side limply, and a look at Preacher's face made Owen gag with sickness. There was a small hole in a cheek, an eye was gone, and there was another small hole square in the middle of his forehead. The back of Preacher's head was wide open. He was covered with blood. Who could have done something like this to him, and why? Owen thoughts raced. He was beginning to feel a deep, angry, sorrow welling up deep inside. Someone was going to pay. Owen carried Preacher to the door of the Social Club. He kicked it open. College Boy, Dinner Roll, and the Paddy rushed over to help. They laid Preacher's body out on a pool table. He was dead. There was no helping him. The room was still. No one knew what to do. The silence was deadly. What was clearly evident was the fact that Owen was about to do something. His face was covered with an incredible, growing, rage that no one knew Owen could even begin to conjure up.

Molly helped Candy up and took her to the women's room to try to clean her up.

In a steely voice that the Carps had never heard before, Owen said to Dinner Roll, "Call 911. Do it now!"

Dinner Roll ran behind the bar and picked up the phone. "It's dead, Owen. It's always dead when we have a dust storm."

Owen said, "Anyone have a cell phone on ya?" No one did. They were so used to two-way radios they didn't use cell phones much.

Owen motioned for Dinner Roll to come over to the pool table. He stood there over Preacher's body with the crew. You could have heard a pin drop in that room.

Owen began, "Now listen, boys, we've got to take care of this ourselves for now. Anyone have guns in their vehicles?"

Cowpaddy said, "I've got two deer rifles, my 22, and a 12 gauge shotgun." Buster, who had left earlier and gone to his trailer for some clandestine reason, had just returned. He couldn't believe all that had happened in the short time he had been gone. When he returned, he came in the back door and found the Club in a complete state of confusion when he walked into the bar area.

He spoke up, sheepishly, and said, "I've got a Glock 9mm under my seat, but if any of you guys tell anyone, I'll go to jail. You guys know I'm on probation for those fights."

Owen said, "Buster, I don't care about that! Preacher is dead! Dammit, boys, go get the guns right now! We've got a job to do."

The boys ran out into the parking lot to Cowpaddy's truck to help him. Buster grabbed his Glock and pulled out a small plastic bag from his shirt pocket. With a frown, he let the contents of the bag blow away in the wind. They all gathered up back inside the Club, and Owen picked up Cowpaddy's Winchester 30-30. He told Paddy to keep the scoped Remington '06. He handed the old 22 rifle to College Boy.

Fortunately, Paddy had a partial box of shells for each deer gun, and a handful of shells for the 22. They were minus a few rounds from recent road hunting, but there were enough to at least make some noise. Dinner Roll grabbed a fire axe from its storage cabinet in corner of the Club.

Owen looked at the crew. They looked ready for whatever was ahead. Each had a look that Owen recognized from his early days of fighting with other soldiers in Iran. They had no fear.

"All right, let's go down to the dirt road and find the bastard!"

They took Candy's Hummer and Preacher's old Ford truck and drove back down the highway. Owen drove the Hummer hard and slid it onto the gravel road, leaving even more of a cloud of dust behind him then the weather had been causing. College Boy and Dinner Roll flew around like rag dolls in the Hummer as Owen managed to stop the SUV suddenly on the road. Owen could see the shadow of the school bus at the edge of the headlight beams of the Hummer. The bus looked totally abandoned.

He said, "There's nobody here; let's go." On a hunch, he wheeled the Hummer on up the dirt road. Cowpaddy and Buster followed behind, the best they could, in the old truck. They kept the Hummer's tail lights in site and tried to keep up in the clouds of dust. The two vehicles roared down the road as fast as they could be driven, bounding through potholes and dodging big rocks.

He could feel his blood heating up. Owen knew he would soon confront whoever killed Preacher.

He said, "We are going to find this guy pretty quickly. There's nowhere for him to hide. There's no place for him to go out here. He can't have gotten far on foot. Let's hope he puts up a fight so we can kill him right off!"

The others sat in silence, knowing there was nothing that could be said that would matter now. Their path was set. They all knew what had to be done.

CHAPTER FIFTEEN

Encounter

THE TRIO ON THE DIRT road heard the Hummer coming.

Mona said, "Samir, Said... get off the road... now!" She jogged off to the left, while Samir and Said headed off to the right. They had no time to get far, as the approaching vehicles were bearing down on them too quickly. The noise of the wind and the darkness and blowing dirt had kept them from realizing how close the oncoming vehicles were until they were almost upon them.

Dinner Roll shouted, "There! There's someone there!" Owen slammed on the Hummer's brakes and slid twenty or thirty yards down the road. They could see someone crouched down in behind a clump of mesquite.

Cowpaddy and Buster pulled in behind the Hummer, not knowing what was going on. They could see two of their friends bailing out of the Hummer, and it was evident they were both looking at something in the brush. College

Boy was still in the front passenger seat, struggling to get the Hummer's door open that had somehow locked in the confusion.

Buster rolled down the window on the truck and shouted, "What's up? What are you guys doing?"

"Hell, Paddy, let's go help them." Buster and Cowpaddy climbed out of the truck.

In that instant, gunfire erupted from the mesquite. Dinner Roll was apparently the largest and easiest target. He was hit immediately in the groin and went down face first into the sand, screaming with pain as the heat from the round burned through his thick thigh like fire. His axe flew out in front of him, landing ahead in the brush.

Samir shouted excitedly, "An axe! They have no weapons! This will be easy! Let's shoot them all down!" Said and Samir opened fire with their automatic rifles. Owen dived for cover. He knew Dinner Roll was down, but there was too much danger of getting shot to get to him.

College Boy shouted out the window of the Hummer, "What the hell! Who are these guys! Dinner Roll, you ok? Owen, what should I do? What should I do?"

At the same time, Buster and Cowpaddy made a dive for better cover. Buster ran into the brush, hoping to get around to the back of the shooters without being detected. Owen opened fire with the Winchester. He didn't have a clear target, but he managed to land a few rounds near the surprised Samir and Said.

College Boy reached for his rifle and fired the 22 cal. out of the Hummer's window, but it seemed more like a toy gun in the middle of the firefight that had ensued. The bolt action of the old rifle was slow and clumsy to operate. Said and Samir backed up a few yards into the darkness as they realized their opponents were armed after all.

Buster could see the muzzle flashes of the automatic rifles, and he worked his way in the brush around the two unsuspecting men. He got in close without being noticed. He was finally close enough that he got down on his hands and knees behind the brush to take a shot. He knew he only had one clip for the Glock and he knew he had to make every shot count. He decided to try to get closer. He got down on all fours and moved toward the men, slowly and quietly. Said and Samir were focused on the men who were already shooting back at them. They had seen Cowpaddy get out of the truck, but hadn't noticed Buster.

Paddy had gotten behind the truck, and stood firing the big deer rifle over the hood in the general direction of the shooters – the scope on the rifle was totally useless in the darkness, but the '06 made a lot of noise when it went off. Paddy thought, Maybe I'll scare them into surrendering.

In the darkness, Buster could finally make out the shapes of Said and Samir. It was hard to judge the distance in the darkness and impossible to aim accurately. He decided to take his shot before he was discovered. He got up on one knee and gripped the Glock with both hands. He pointed the barrel at the nearest figure and waited for the next series of muzzle flashes to be as sure as he could of his target.

Just then, Samir raked both the Hummer and the old Ford truck with bullets, hoping to cause an explosion that would take out one or two of the enemy. Cowpaddy knelt down behind the truck, trying to avoid being hit. The truck shuddered with the bullets riddling its sides and shattering its windshield. College Boy was still inside the Hummer and as he heard the rounds ripping into the sides of the SUV he began screaming for help.

Flying glass hit Cowpaddy in the face as he tried to get back from the truck. He finally stumbled into the brush behind him, feeling the wetness of blood trickling down his check. It was a fortunate move, because just as he went down, Samir pitched a grenade that landed just between the Hummer and the Ford. The explosion immediately set the Hummer ablaze, lighting up the entire area. Cowpaddy suddenly stood out like a sore thumb in the glare, and Samir stood up and fired at him. A round smashed into the scope on the Remington, sending pieces of it into Cowpaddy's face and neck. He was a bloody mess by now and couldn't see out of his left eye.

After the grenade went off, and Samir and Said resumed their firing at Owen and kept him pinned down. Owen tried several times to get up to go over to the Hummer to help College Boy, but every time he tried, automatic rifle fire put him back down in the dirt.

Buster could finally see enough muzzle flashes and movement, and the outlines of the men were just barely visible. Buster said to himself, They aren't twenty yards away. An easy shot for the Glock. In the wind and dirt, they were probably closer than they appeared to be. But it didn't matter. It was time to try to take them out. Buster aimed at the figure of the nearest man, fired three or four quick shots, and dived for cover.

Said screamed with pain as two of Buster's rounds hit him in the side and hip. He rolled over behind a clump of mesquite, dropping his rifle and grabbing his side. Samir turned and fired in Buster's general direction. He couldn't see anyone, so his shots were wild. He grabbed Said's arm and pulled him further back into the brush away from whoever had shot him. Said mumbled something to Samir and squeezed his hand for a moment. He quickly slipped into unconsciousness. Samir let his brother collapse under the brush. A pool of dark blood gathered underneath him. Samir knew what he had to do. His brother was surely lost. He reached into his pack for a grenade, pulled the pin, and put it carefully under Said. He said a short prayer for his brother and moved off into the darkness, firing a few shots toward where he thought Buster was, as he fled. Samir had no idea where Mona had gone, so he just kept moving, hoping to run into her.

Buster felt himself trying to push completely flat into the sand and rocks. He could hear the automatic weapon firing and could literally feel the rounds zipping past him just above his body. As soon as Samir stopped firing, Buster scrambled silently to a different spot to wait for his next chance. But, there was no more firing. Not even Owen and the others back on the road were firing. It was deadly quiet, except for the popping and snapping sounds coming from the burning Hummer.

Deciding that the shooters had left, he stood and walked over to where he saw them last, hoping to find a blood trail. There, under a mesquite bush, lay a man in a pool of blood. He wasn't moving.

Buster shouted at Owen, "Hey, I got one of the bastards. He looks like he's dead. Owen, are you okay over there?"

Owen knew right away that Buster was in the wrong place at the wrong time. He remembered so many friends lost the same way in Iraq.

He shouted back, "Buster...wait! Don't move!"

It was too late. Buster had walked over to Said, pointed his handgun towards his head, and kicked his body over with his boot to see if he was alive. The grenade rolled out from under him and exploded.

CHAPTER SIXTEEN

A Mother's Fear

JANCI CARPENTER pulled into the parking lot of the Social Club. She knew that was where she'd find Roy. He was her only son – her pride and joy. He'd be in the bar drinking with the crew like he was most evenings. Janci was an attractive woman in her early 50's. Preacher used to tell Owen, in private, that Janci was his view of the typical well-healed Texas woman. He said she had "a bad case of the Texas too's ... she's too blond, her jeans are way too tight, she wears too much makeup, too much perfume, and too much gold jewelry." She had a very small frame, but a temper that was fiery enough to make even the toughest roughneck cringe in fear. The men often called her "little dynamite" when Dinner Roll wasn't around. She ran a tight ship, with Carpenter Gas and Oil. He was her business, lock, stock, and barrel, and she fought to keep it together.

Her late husband, "Toad" Hammond, had, with Janci's smart mind and his strong back, built the organization up from scratch before he managed to get himself killed in a dumb, drunken mistake that not only cost him his life but the lives of two other men on one of the back-country rigs.

Janci liked Owen. She trusted him to control the crew, manage the operations in the field, and to make sure she made money. And, on top of that, he was, she thought, cute. She liked young, rugged, good looking men, and was often seen in Midland's nightspots with one tucked under her arm.

She opened the door of the Social Club and instantly saw Preacher's body stretched out on a pool table. Her first thought was that he had passed out drunk. She glanced over to one of the bar's few booths and saw Molly sitting there trying to console the clearly devastated Candy, who was leaning against the wall side of the booth, sobbing and shaking. She looked back at Preacher and saw blood. Lots of blood.

"My God! What on earth is going on!" Janci shouted.

Molly motioned her over. She said, "There's been a terrible shooting. Preacher has been killed. Owen took the Carps out to find the man who did it. They've been gone half an hour or so. I'm really worried about them. And Janci, Roy's with them. With this damned storm, we can't get a phone line out to contact the Pecos County Sheriff. The boys decided to take care of it themselves, and they took guns."

Janci went over to the booth and sat

down. She looked dazed. After a moment, she collected herself and said flatly, "We'll, we just need to get out there and help them ourselves. I don't want Roy hurt! He's all I have left that matters in this world."

Molly couldn't believe Janci would even suggest such a thing, even though she understood how a mother might feel about the safety of her only son. The simple fact was that Janci just didn't seem the type to want to go to the brush, no matter what the reason. The idea of her running around in the sand and rocks, in her $800 Vivier shoes, let alone in the dark and in the middle of a wind storm, was simply a lot to fathom.

"If we can't get the law here until this storm blows through, we have to take some initiative! They may need our help. We just can't sit here doing nothing!" Janci said, almost as if she were trying to convince herself.

Candy was finally calming down, and she stood up and walked over to Preacher's body and picked up his cold, stiffening, hand. She held it just for a moment. She turned and pulled a red checkered table cloth off the nearest table, letting the beer bottles and plates crash to the floor. She covered Preacher's face, and turned to look at Molly and Janci.

She said, "Janci's right. Let's go find them. They may need our help. I don't want to lose any more of the boys. Let's get going."

The trio walked out of the Club and strode deliberately into the parking lot to Janci's car.

Janci said, "I'll drive." They climbed into her new gold Lexus and pulled quickly out of the parking lot to the edge of the highway.

Janci said, "Where were they, Candy? Which way do we go?"

Candy gathered her thoughts and said, "Head on down the highway to the right. There's an abandoned school bus not far ahead that's pulled off to the side of the road just next to the service road. I don't think we can miss the bus. It was on fire. The crew will be there, or near there. That's where someone shot Preach. He didn't have a chance, Janci. He just wanted to help!"

CHAPTER SEVENTEEN

One Man Standing

OWEN KNEW College Boy was dead. There had been nothing he could do to save him. He couldn't get to him. His screams had finally stopped and the Hummer was totally engulfed in flames. And, he also knew Buster was dead. He tried to warn him. He'd seen the whole scenario before in Iraq, too many times. He knew that the explosion meant that Buster had fallen for the same old trick that had killed so many others.

As he crammed more shells from his pocket into the magazine of the Winchester, he walked cautiously over toward Buster. Sure enough, the trunk of Buster's body was lying there, next to another dead man. Buster must have been close, he thought.

Obviously, the other shooter had escaped into the brush. At least he thought there had been two of them. He bent over and carefully picked up Buster's Glock handgun. It still had a few rounds in the clip, so he shoved the gun into his belt and turned to go back to see what, if anything, he could do for Dinner Roll and Cowpaddy.

Dinner Roll was in bad shape. He was on the ground holding his groin. His jeans were soaked. It was clear he had lost a lot of blood and was in very severe pain. Owen pulled off his leather belt and put it around the upper leg, tightening it as much as Dinner Roll could stand. Dinner Roll was moaning and seemed to be growing more and more incoherent by the moment.

"Owen, it hurts! I don't know what happened...I don't know how to make it stop hurting...why did they do this? What did I do wrong?"

Owen said, "Roy, hold the belt tight or you'll bleed to death."

Roy reached down pulled on the end of belt and clinched his teeth as the pain increased. He was scared.

Owen then went over to Cowpaddy, who was sitting upright on the ground behind the truck. His face was bloody and he was in a daze. One of his eyes was badly damaged. Owen asked, "How you doin' buddie?"

Cowpaddy sat silently. At a glance, Owen decided he wasn't critically wounded. Maybe in shock, he thought.

Owen wanted to see if he could get to College Boy's body. He stood up and walked over to the burning vehicle. He tried to get close enough to the Hummer to look inside, but it was simply too hot. The bright yellow paint was gone and the SUV's body was blackened from the flames and heat. The windows had all blown out and flames licked out in darkness like angry demons. He knew there would not be much left to identify College Boy. The heat had been too intense.

He turned and went over to the old truck, remembering that Preacher always had a first aid kit under the seat. The windshield and side windows were blown out, and glass was strewn all over the cab's seats and floorboards. He carefully reached under the seat until he found the kit. Owen took the kit over to where Cowpaddy was sitting. He opened it and took out a compress bandage, and put it over Cowpaddy's eye.

He picked up Cowpaddy's hand and put it over the bandage, saying "Keep your hand on this, boy."

Owen thought, This is too much like war. Automatic weapons, grenades, in west Texas? These guys knew what they were doing. They took advantage of a bunch of guys who weren't killers. These men were professionals. It's too much! It makes absolutely no sense.

Then it hit him like a lightning bolt. The man on the ground next to Buster...looked like an Iraqi! He is definitely Middle Eastern. What the hell are they doing here, and why here? What could possibly....." he wondered. Then it struck him, "They are after the oil and gas fields – there's no other reason!" Owen knew he had to stop them.

CHAPTER EIGHTEEN

Mona

SHE HAD MADE her way a half mile or so away from the gunfire, maybe farther. Mona had seen two sets of headlights coming up the road. She didn't know who they were, or how many of them there were, but she knew there had been plenty of shooting. She could clearly hear Said and Samir's AK47's in the darkness, in spite of the wind. They had their own special sound. And, she could hear the heavy rifle fire and the pistol fire. The explosion of the grenade was unmistakable. The darkness had revealed the glowing fire from a vehicle. Mona knew that the brothers had done damage. She knew they'd fight to the death if need be, and she assumed they had and that she was now alone with the task ahead of her of setting off the lethal bomb she carried. Mona was ready to die for Jihad and for Allah and she had been convinced for days that this was a one-way mission. Allah had saved her for this, and she found what she felt was a wonderful irony that it was these hated Americans who had foolishly saved her in that hospital. They had saved her so that she could continue to serve Allah and carry the Jihad to Texas.

She knelt down to check her equipment. She carried the priceless suitcase containing the cesium bomb, two sticks of dynamite, a Glock, and an AK47 with a few extra clips. She had no food and no water. She was thirsty. The wind had driven so much dust and dirt into her eyes, and as a result they itched incessantly. She could taste the grit and grime of the desert in her mouth. It reminded her of home...of Iraq...all very familiar.

She stood and began walking back toward the gravel service road. Mona knew she could explode the device anywhere in the area and it would contaminate the wells for a great many miles around for a long time to come. The question was to find just the right spot. She and Fadia had talked about that on the bus ride up to the Permian Basin...the right spot. They hoped to fit the bombs to well sites to be sure of destroying at least one rig. Ideally, they wanted to find pumping stations for maximum disruption. In the darkness, and in the wind, it was difficult to see far enough around in any direction to spot oil or gas equipment. It was going to have to be pure luck to stumble upon the perfect spot, but it had to be on the service road. She circled back toward the road, but away from the burning vehicle. Mona knew if she kept walking, sooner or later she'd find the right place. She had to be there before the storm ended, and before the sun rose in west Texas. She hurried as quickly as she could, stumbling forward over the rocks and brush in the darkness of the night.

CHAPTER NINETEEN

Luck of Allah

ASHUR, FADIA, AND Bernardo trotted across the highway after leaving the bus and headed into the desert. The wind was at their back as they pushed forward into the darkness. Their clothing blew in their faces and they sometimes felt pulled along by the storm. They hadn't gotten far when they heard the distant shooting and explosions in the air. They knew something had gone amiss, and they knew it was likely up to them to do as much damage to the wells as they could.

Bernardo was reluctant from the beginning. It was only Ashur's threat that kept him with them. Otherwise, he would have begun walking south toward Mexico. This wasn't his fight or his Jihad. He was in it for the money. He knew he was to be paid at the end of the journey, and he suspected Ashur carried the money he was supposed to receive. Along with Ashur threatening to shoot him, the money was a very good reason to take his chances in going along. It beat the certainty of death in not going. He carried a pack with food and water, as well as extra ammunition and grenades.

They eventually came upon the gravel service road that Ashur and Fadia knew was there. They thought it would take them to a well site. It seemed recently used and fairly well maintained. So, they took the road and walked for a mile or so until they arrived at exactly the kind of site they were looking for.

There it was. A small gas compression station reared up in the darkness just ahead of them, with the humps of its silvery pipes rising like huge, unmoving, reptilian creatures in the windy, night sky.

Ashur said, "What luck! This is exactly what we were looking for. We can do a lot of damage with the explosion, and contaminate the area at the same time. Perfect!" Fadia agreed, "Yes, exactly. Let's get to our job. I'm worried we are going to be interrupted by people looking for the man we shot. They are bound to come, sooner or later. Bernardo, keep a sharp eye out. It is your job to warn us if anyone approaches. We won't need long to do this."

They walked over to the station and looked over the area. The site was surrounded by a sea of darkness, and there was obviously no one around. There was no fence. Only a couple of small buildings stood on the site. It was almost too easy. They quickly spread their equipment out on the ground. Ashur found a fuse box on a pole next to one of the buildings and flipped on a small night light. Fadia pulled out the suitcase and walked over to the center of the station's central machinery. She set the suitcase down next to a set of large pipes arching out of a concrete pad. She sat down and opened up the box. The cesium was encased and secured it its own small container. She took the two sticks of dynamite she carried and taped them to the cesium's shiny aluminum housing. She laid one end of the fuse next to the dynamite.

"I won't use caps. I'll just ignite the fuse. It will be simple," she said to herself. She then used her knife to carve an opening in the side of the suitcase for the fuse, ran it through, and closed the case.

Fadia turned to Ashur and said, "It's nearly ready. We have fifty feet of fuse. It will not allow much time to get away. We will have to make a run for it."

Ashur found himself thinking of Lisa at that moment. He wanted to see her again, and wanted to enjoy Austin just one more time. He had hoped they would set their bombs, run down the service road toward the highway. If they could get far enough, quickly enough, they might have the luck to find transportation and escape back to Mexico. The bus was useless. The only hope they had was to find something new. They simply had to get back to the blacktop, and then maybe they could get to the lights up the road and steal a vehicle.

He responded, "Good, Fadia. Nicely done.

Now, let's plan the escape before you ignite the fuse."

Fadia looked at him with disgust, and retorted, "You worry me, Ashur. All you think about is how to save yourself. First things first. We have to do this, Ashur. Let me finish. We can't, as the killer American president always says, 'cut and run.' We have come a long way for this job. We have to accomplish our mission, Ashur. You must be strong! If Allah intends it, we will find our way out of here. Let me get this fuse lit first, and then we'll find our way out of here."

Fadia found herself reaching under her coat and placing her hand on the Glock. She sensed Ashur was growing weak. She sensed he was about to run and she knew she might have to kill him. She knew the truth. There was no way to escape in time.

"Fadia, I'm not saying we cut and run. I'm saying we need a plan. We won't have time to think once that fuse is lit. We need to look for transportation to get us out of here. Relax!"

Bernardo sensed that things were beginning to unravel. He had been backing up toward the mesquite that surrounded the compression station as this conversation unfolded. He didn't like the sound of the discussion, and he knew his value to the mission was now very minimal.

He spoke up, "My friends, I can go find a vehicle and come for you. I could go to the lights, get a car or truck, and be back here in just a few minutes. I could go now. Let me take care of this. No problem. I'll be right back. Just wait a minute." Bernardo kept backing up. He had a look of fear and panic on his face. His eyes were wide, gleaming in the dim light. He stumbled over a rock and fell backwards.

Fadia wheeled toward Bernardo, pulled her Glock, and fired at him as he struggled to stand up, hitting him several times in his midsection. Bernardo again stumbled back a few feet and fell to the ground, clutching his stomach. He rolled away into the darkness. Fadia knew she'd hit him and decided to let him die in the desert. She said, "It's what he deserves – a miserable death. He'll never survive a stomach wound, unless he has the luck of Allah to save him."

CHAPTER TWENTY

Picking up the Pieces

THE LEXUS TURNED onto the gravel next to the school bus. They could see the fire burning down the road, so they drove towards the light.

Molly, feeling a deep fear for Owen, said "Janci, you're driving like a little old lady...get on it! We've got to get to them!"

As they got closer, they could see the burning hulk of what was once Candy's prized yellow Hummer. She could see the smoldering fire from the back seat.

"Oh my God! What the hell happened!" she said. They pulled in behind Preacher's truck and got out. Owen had seen them coming and walked quickly over to them. He didn't want them looking into the Hummer.

"Janci, now be calm...Roy's going to be all right, but you've got to get him to the hospital right away. He and Cowpaddy have been shot. Buster and College Boy are both dead. College Boy is in the Hummer, Janci. He's gone. Don't go over there."

"Roy!" Janci ran over to where Dinner Roll was lying. He was covered with blood and at first, she couldn't tell where he was hit.

She said, "Roy, how bad is it?" Dinner Roll didn't respond. His eyes were glazed and his body was shaking. He still had hold of the end of the belt that was tight around his wounded thigh.

Owen, with a deeply worried look said, "He's going into shock, Janci. You've got to get him and Cowpaddy out of here. On top of that, this isn't over by a long way. You've got to go get some help, dammit! Something big is going on here that has to do with the gas wells."

He bent down and struggled to get Cowpaddy up. He and Janci helped him over to the Lexus.

"Janci, open this damned tailgate and lay that back seat down!" Janci opened the rear hatch and went around to the side door to lay the rear seat flat. Owen sat Cowpaddy into the back of the Lexus and then went to help get Dinner Roll. It took all of them to pick him up, but they did it. He was a big boy. They managed to get him into the back next to Cowpaddy. They couldn't get the hatch closed.

Owen finally said, "Hell, just leave it up. Someone sit back here and keep them from falling out!" No one moved.

In a nervous voice, Owen said, "Ok, Janci, you, Candy, and Molly - get them out of here!"

Molly looked at Owen and got up close to him, staring directly into his eyes. She said, "If you think I'm leaving you here, you've got another think coming. Candy needs to go with Janci, but I'm staying."

At that, Candy stepped up and challenged them both, "Hardly. I'm staying. There's payback comin' and I'm going to be a part of that!"

"Well, hell," said Janci, "We've got to get out of here right now. I'm getting Roy to the hospital. Now listen, I'll get help back here as soon as I can. Don't no one else get hurt! You guys help me get them in enough to close the hatch. They managed to get it done and Janci climbed into the Lexus, turned it around, and headed off back towards the blacktop.

Owen gathered up the rifles, gave Candy the Remington, and walked over to Preacher's truck. He brushed as much of the glass as he could off the seat and got in. He turned on the key and the old Ford started right up. Its windshield was gone, but it was running. "Watch out for the glass, Molly," Owen said, as Molly stepped in on the passenger side. Candy climbed into the bed of the truck, with the rifle in her hands.

She leaned over the top of the cab and hollered, "Let's go, Owen!"

Owen handed Molly the Winchester and told her to keep her eyes open. The three of them headed off into the brush after the other shooter, Samir. Owen knew he had to find a way to keep the women from getting hurt. They were dealing with a professional killer. He knew the killer was likely going to be suicidal and would love to take all of them with him if he could. Owen kept thinking and wondering what these people had been up to, and he worried that if there were more than these two men out there, they might be in for it.

CHAPTER TWENTY-ONE

The Rundown

IT WASN'T BUT a few minutes of bouncing along in the desert that the headlights flashed on someone running ahead of the truck. The runner cut to the right and tried to get behind the brush. Candy fired first, three or four times, emptying the Remington. The runner turned and fired back with his automatic rifle, but missed his mark entirely, kicking up dirt and rocks around the truck. He stood up and kept running away from the truck.

Owen gunned the Ford and shouted, "Hang on, you two! This is going to get rough."

Candy replied, "Get him! Get the bastard!"

Molly fired the Winchester twice, and managed to hit the runner with the second shot plowing into his lower leg. The impact of the bullet knocked him sprawling into the dirt, and his weapon went flying into the air. Owen drove the Ford right at him. Samir tried to stand, reaching frantically for the Glock that was tucked into his waistband. He pulled up the gun to attempt to fire just as the truck reached him. Owen ran him down as he pulled the trigger and fired a shot uselessly into the air. Preacher's truck dragged him underneath the front end thirty or forty yards into the brush before Owen hit the brakes and let the truck slow to a stop. The man screamed at first, but soon stopped.

They got out and went around to the front of the truck. Candy had the Remington ready, pointing it toward the man who was caught under the truck. They looked under the truck, and evidently Samir's clothing had tangled and caught in the cross member and suspension under the Ford's front end. He was clearly dying, but still alive. The skin was completely gone from his lower arms, hands, and from his exposed legs. His shoes had been ripped off and one of his feet was completely torn off. A large section of his scalp rested against the exhaust system and his hair and skin were sizzling.

Smells like a burnt hamburger, thought Owen. The skin and hair clung to the hot, rusted, metal and he couldn't pull loose. The hair and skin continued to smoke and stink.

Candy stuck the barrel of the Remington into Samir's cheek, ready to blow him into his paradise at the slightest movement.

Owen said, "Wait." He leaned next to Samir as closely as he could and said, "Tell us how many of you there are and we won't kill you."

Samir didn't speak. He stared back with a look of pure hatred and contempt.   Owen said, "Tell us now, or we'll drag you another hundred yards just like this, until you come apart at the joints!" Samir mumbled something familiar, in Arabic that Owen knew essentially meant "Go to hell."

He pushed Candy back and said, "Let's wait a bit. He's just not fully cooked."

Owen walked back behind the truck a ways until he found the AK47 that Samir had lost, and he found the bag Samir had been carrying containing spare clips and another hand grenade. He walked back to the truck. Candy was down on her knees staring into Samir's eyes.

She turned and looked back to see Owen and said, "Owen, he just called me Fadia, or something like that. I think there are others here."

Candy looked back at Samir. She had a look on her face that Owen would always remember, and one that he didn't ever want to see again. She shoved the Remington's barrel roughly into Samir's mouth.

Owen said, "Wait, Candy," but at just that moment, she fired. Samir's head exploded under the truck, and blood, sand and rocks splattered out in all directions.   Candy stood up, looking down at the body and said, "That's for Preach, you bastard!"

Owen stooped down and reached under the truck and cut Samir's clothing away from the cross member.

He stood up and said, "Get in. We're going to take a look around."

Owen backed the truck up, crushing Samir's body with one of the front tires, leaving the young Syrian broken and bloodied behind in the red Texas dust.

Molly said, "Owen, how do we know what direction to go?"

Owen replied, "We go the opposite direction. I'm guessing that those two were decoys. They were intended to keep us away from something they didn't want us to catch up to."

He wheeled the Ford around and headed back. Candy had taken her position again in the bed of the truck, leaning over the cab with the Remington pointing ahead. Molly stuck the Winchester out across the hood through the open windshield, scanning the area revealed by the headlights. The wind was still howling, and dust and dirt was blowing into their eyes. It was difficult to make out very much ahead. They drove across the gravel road, passing near to the smoldering skeleton of the Hummer, and whatever was left of College Boy still inside.

CHAPTER TWENTY-TWO

An Unexpected Coup

FADIA TURNED and stared at Ashur. She pointed the AK47 towards him and he knew she wouldn't have the slightest reservation in shooting him too. Ashur didn't know quite what to do. He couldn't tell what she was going to do next. He could see what she was thinking. He finally took a risk to try and buy some time.

He looked straight at Fadia and said, "Bernardo was our ticket out of here, Fadia! What are you doing? We needed him to find the way! Now we need to think of something else."

In a voice that seemed almost disconnected from her body, Fadia said, "You are no longer in charge here, Ashur. You never were, little boy. Either join me right now to accomplish our mission, or die. You decide. I need your help, but I can do this without you."

Again, Ashur couldn't find the right words. It was clear, however, that Fadia meant exactly what she said.

121

He didn't want to die, so he said, "Fadia, I have no problem with what you've said. I'll help. We'll get this thing done together for the Jihad...and for Allah." He wanted to mention that they would then find their way out, but he figured she's shoot him, so he stopped with that. Fadia lowered her weapon.

"Take the fuse, Ashur, and unwrap it. We need to take it as far out into the brush as it will stretch before we light it. Stretched fuses burn more quickly. The storm is beginning to die down and daylight is going to be upon us. We have to move quickly."

Ashur took the fuse strand and unraveled it. He walked with it back away from the pumping station several yards. Fadia busied herself with double-checking the suitcase, making sure the fuse remained connected to the dynamite. The cesium would not ignite without an explosion from the dynamite.

Ashur suddenly made a decision. He knew the only chance he had to escape and to live was to kill Fadia, and he knew he had to do it right now. He slowly unslung his AK47 without her noticing. She was focused on the dynamite and the cesium bomb. He had only a brief moment to his own devices, but the time was just long enough for him to manage to raise the rifle and point it at her.

He shouted, "Fadia, stand up and drop your weapons. Now!"

Fadia looked up in shock and surprise.

She said, "I didn't think you had the

backbone, Ashur. I thought you were too weak to finish this mission. I thought you'd be too weak to challenge me. It looks like I was wrong. So you are going to betray your people and the Jihad? You are selling out to the Americans? We've come all this way for nothing because you are a coward?"

"You are wrong, Fadia. I was always going to finish this mission. I just wanted to live beyond it. Can't you understand that? I just wanted to make sure we had a chance to survive. We could have done it."

Fadia stood up. Ashur hesitated, not knowing what she was going to do. Suddenly she dived for cover, rolling away from Ashur. She picked up her rifle on the roll. She stood back up and aimed at him just as he fired. He squeezed the trigger and unloaded his clip. When it was empty, he lowered his weapon and walked over to Fadia's quiet body. Unfortunately he had missed her, entirely. She suddenly rose up, pointed her weapon at Ashur, and fired a short burst. She had killed before. Ashur had not. This made the difference just now.

She killed Ashur instantly.

CHAPTER TWENTY-THREE

Woman to Woman

MONA HAD FINALLY found the outline of the well-site in the darkness. She was making her way over to it when her foot slipped into a narrow, but deep, crevice in the ground. She gasped with pain at a loud snapping sound of her ankle breaking. She had managed, in the darkness, to step into an opening in the rough Texas terrain that ran alongside a buried gas line. Her foot was wedged, and the pain from the broken ankle was nearly unbearable. It was time to take an accounting of her situation. She laid her suitcase down in front of her, and unslung her AK47. In her back pack she had two sticks of dynamite, extra clips, her Glock, and a grenade.

Then, over the noise of the wind, she heard the truck approaching. She looked back the way she had just come and there it was, bouncing over rocks and mesquite, heading directly at her. She reached over for the AK47, chambered a fresh round, and waited for the truck to get closer.

These stupid Texans. They don't see me. I'll kill them all easily and have a vehicle to use to finish this, she thought as she tried to flatten herself against the ground. She said to herself, Remember, Mona...no silhouette...remember your training. They won't see you unless you show them your silhouette.

Candy leaned down to the window and shouted to Owen, "You know there's a gas well ahead. It's the one we had to put the temporary cap on last week. Maybe they are heading that way."

Owen remembered. He drove the truck in the general direction he thought they'd find the well. The road to it came in from the south, so they wouldn't strike it. They'd just have to luck into it.

Molly shouted, "There it is! I see it, just ahead!"

Owen and Candy saw it too. Candy's voice was getting horse from shouting over the noise of the truck and wind, but she did her best. "There's no one here...I can't see anyone! We should have gone the other way!"

No sooner had Molly spoken, Mona opened fire on the truck. Bullets struck the grill and front bumper, and then hit the only remaining headlight. Owen had pressed down on the accelerator to try to get them away when he hit a large rock, causing the truck to leap into the air and then come crashing down with a powerful jolt. Owen's head smashed against the steel roof of the truck and he was knocked unconscious. Molly reached over for the wheel and steered the truck away from the shooter. She jammed her foot down on the gas and they moved away from Mona's line of fire.

Candy had managed to hang on, and turned to shoot the big Remington. She ripped off four rounds toward Mona, and ducked down to reload.

Mona fired another clip at the truck as it moved away from her, but it was far enough away that her shots missed the mark completely. She emptied a clip, popped it out, and snapped in a fresh one, ready to fire at the first opportunity.

The truck came to a stop and the women climbed out to assess the damage. Owen was out cold.

Candy said, "Molly, we have to do this ourselves. You move back toward the shooter and I'll circle completely around and come in from behind him. Don't shoot me, Molly, and stay down low, ok? Get out there and take cover. Fire a couple of rounds to get his attention. He won't be expecting me."

Molly took the Winchester, shoved in shells until it wouldn't take any more. She turned and headed back toward the shooter.

Candy took off running. She's tough, Molly thought. I didn't know she was in such good shape! She can really run for as big as she is! Then she smiled to herself. Stupid me. What am I saying? She hunkered down as low as she could and moved slowly through the mesquite, keeping as much brush between herself and the enemy.

Candy moved across the desert like she belonged out there. She leaped over bushes and rocks, soundlessly. She circled out around the well-site and came back in from behind. She knew, if they were lucky and there was only one shooter, that they had whoever it was in between them.

Mona cursed to herself for getting her foot caught. What bad fortune. Allah help me! She jerked and twisted, trying to get free. The more she pulled, the more she was trapped.

Then it came to her. I've got to explode the bomb, right here and now. She pulled the suitcase over to her and opened it up. The cesium bomb looked to be in good condition. She reached for a stick of dynamite and taped it to the case, next to the cesium container. Just as she began searching through the backpack for the fuse, she heard Molly in the brush ahead of her. Just as Candy planned, Molly fired a shot in the air as she moved forward.

Mona picked up the AK and waited for her to come into sight. Molly wasn't certain where the enemy was hiding. She just had a good idea, and she tried to move in the right direction. She thought she'd gone far enough, and found a shallow depression in the ground. She got down on her stomach and fired another shot into the air.

There . . . I see you, Mona said to herself as

she spotted the muzzle flash of the Winchester. She could see movement as Molly slowly looked over the top of the depression. Mona aimed the AK47. As she was about to squeeze the trigger, something struck her in the back of the head. Suddenly, there was only blackness.

Candy had tried to shoot her from a distance, but realized she had lost the clip from the Remington while she ran. She was completely out of ammunition. She had the perfect shot. She aimed along side of the broken scope and had what she now realized was a woman dead in her sights. When she pulled the trigger, there was only a soft click. Thankfully, the shooter hadn't heard the click, because of the wind, and Molly had her totally distracted. Candy was able to creep up behind her and she swung the stock of the Remington as hard as she could, hitting the woman in the back of the head and knocking her cold.

Molly had foolishly looked up over the brush just in time to see the woman aiming at her and, just in time, Candy swinging her gun. She knew it had been a close call. She stood up and ran over to Candy. They both looked down at the woman.

"What the hell is this? What's all this crap? And what the hell, a woman? She looks like a Middle Eastern woman," said Candy.

As she kicked the guns away from Mona, she noticed the Glock handgun. She remembered then. It was the gun she saw pointing at Preacher. "This is the one that killed

Preacher. The bitch! We need to take care of her real special like, Molly."

Molly looked up at Candy. Candy had the strangest look in her eyes.

"I'll go get Owen and the truck," Molly said. She found Owen still unconscious behind the wheel of the truck. Molly pulled him over so that she could get behind the wheel. She drove over to Candy and her trophy and got out of the truck.

"Molly, look at this suitcase," Candy said. She had been going through the backpack and spotted the wooden container. She opened it and discovered what she assumed was an explosive device. "It's a bomb. On the metal casing inside the suitcase it's marked 'cesium.' She was going to blow up the well-site. More than that, Molly, I think that this is a dirty bomb!" She bent down and carefully untaped the dynamite, closed up the case, and put it on the floorboard on the passenger side of the truck. They gathered up the grenades, dynamite, the Glock, and the AK47 and put them in the bed of the truck.

Then they went back to get Mona. Blood was dripping from the gash the Remington's stock had caused on the back of her head. Her hair was soaked in blood, but she was breathing. Candy reached down, grabbed hold of her arms and pulled her up. "Dammit, her foot's caught, Molly!" Candy said, and then decided, Who cares? as she pulled as hard as she could, snapping Mona's ankle and popping it out of the crevice. Mona groaned with pain,

but didn't wake up. Candy dragged her over
to the truck and literally threw her like a rag
doll onto the floor of the cab on the passenger
side.   Molly watched Candy with disbelief. She
was amazingly strong.

"She isn't waking up for awhile, Molly,
don't worry. Get in. Let's get back to the Social
Club."

CHAPTER TWENTY-FOUR

Latin Love

IN ALL THE COMMOTION between Ashur and Fadia, Bernardo had managed to get to his feet and run off into the brush. His stomach was on fire and he knew if he didn't get help soon that he was likely going to be a dead man. He stumbled toward the blacktop, trying to get as far away from the shooting as he could. He kept mumbling, "crazy bastards!" He knew someone would be after him as soon as they realized he was still alive. It was a struggle to walk. Bernardo knew he'd been hit more than once. As he struggled along, he glanced down and noticed his brass belt buckle may have saved him, since it had a prominent dent in it now. "Holy Mary, Mother of Jesus!" he said outloud, and he kept running.

Just as Bernardo reached the highway he saw the headlights of a vehicle heading his way. It was Candy, Molly, and Owen, and their passenger. Candy slammed on the brakes and Molly jumped out with the Winchester pointed at the man.

He said, in the most pitiful voice, "Help me, please!"

Molly could see he was badly wounded, bleeding, and unarmed. She led him over to the back of the truck. He looked in and saw the weapons.

He backed up from the truck, saying "I don't have anything to do with this!" Candy jumped out of the truck and grabbed Bernardo by the arm.

She said, "Listen, you bastard, are there more of you out here? You better damn well tell me right now or we'll shoot you again in the stomach and let you bleed to death at the side of the road!"

Bernardo flinched, as Candy smacked him, open-handed, alongside his head. "Tell us now!" she screamed.

Bernardo said, "All right—yes, there are more. They are over there by the machinery." He pointed back into the brush.

Candy looked at Molly and said, "They are after the pumping station. If they have another one of these dirty bombs, we are all going to die. Come on, get in the truck!" Candy shoved Bernardo out of the way. "We'll come back for you. Don't go anywhere."

Candy drove the truck off of the highway into the brush and headed cross country toward the pumping station. She looked at Molly and said, "Better get that rifle ready. Be sure the damned thing is loaded. We may not have much time when we get there. It's just over this little rise ahead!"

Owen was finally starting to rouse, but was a long ways from being coherent. He bounced back and forth between the woman and they both tried to keep him from hitting the dashboard. Mona was on the floor in front of Molly. Molly reached through the sliding back window of the truck and managed to get the AK47 into the cab. She looked it over and decided it seemed pretty simple to operate. She pulled the bolt back to slam a shell into the chamber. She popped out the clip. It looked like it was nearly full, so she popped it back in until it clicked.

"All those action movies I had to watch with Owen finally paid off, Candy," she joked. "A little black humor. Sorry."

The truck rolled forward over the rocks and over the mesquite toward the pumping station.

CHAPTER TWENTY-FIVE

The Wild Hog

AS THEY NEARED the pumping station, Candy stopped the truck. The wind was still blowing, but nothing like it was earlier. She knew if something was going to happen, it would be very soon. Daylight was almost upon them and the storm was subsiding.

She said, "Molly, let's get out and do the same drill we did on the other one." Molly nodded and they got out of the truck. Just as Candy stepped out, a wild Javalina jumped up from where it had been lying. It squealed and ran toward the pumping station. "Jesus! That damned pig scared the crap out of me!" Candy said.

Candy grabbed the AK47 from Molly.

She said, "Take the Winchester and that pistol. I'll meet you in the middle. This time, be a little more careful, darlin'. I don't want you dead too!"

Candy took off running, just like before. She was going to make a wide circle around to the rear of the facility.

Molly worked the lever action on the Winchester to make sure it was loaded. There looked to be a round in the chamber. It was ready. And, she looked at the pistol and pulled the slide back. It had a round in the chamber. She managed to eject the clip to see if it was full. It was, so off she went.

As Molly approached the pumping station, she could see absolutely nothing moving. The wind and dust was blowing across the site and visibility was very poor. Tumbleweeds rolled by her one after another, and she knew that the pig was somewhere ahead too. She hoped she didn't run into it. That was the last thing she needed, she thought. She finally got down on the ground and began crawling forward. She wondered where Candy was. It had seemed like more than enough time for her to be behind the site.

CHAPTER TWENTY-SIX

Whenever Yer Plannin' the Devil's a'Laughin'

MONA WAS FRANTIC. She couldn't find a match to light the fuse. She had managed to firmly attach the fuse to the dynamite. It was ready. She frantically tore open her backpack. No matches. She was sure they were there when she was on the bus. She had checked, and double checked. Where are they! she said to herself, over and over. They must be here somewhere.

No matches. Then she remembered that Ashur had a backpack. She stood up to walk over to his body when she saw something moving towards her in the mesquite. She picked up her rifle and fired several rounds. The Javilina squealed and ran around in circles until it collapsed.

A miserable pig? Why a pig out here? she thought. She had apparently hit it in the head.

Candy heard the shooting and assumed Molly was in a firefight with whoever was there.

She ran hard toward the pumping station. As she reached the site, she could see someone bent over a body. It was Mona. She had her hands on the little plastic box of matches that she's pulled from Ashur's pack. As she stood up, her eyes met Candy's eyes. They both stood there for what seemed like an eternity, staring at one another. Mona quickly glanced over at the suitcase. Candy's eyes followed her. In that instant, Mona raised her rifle and fired at Candy. The rounds hit Candy's rifle, knocking it out of her hands. She dived for cover behind a huge pipe. Mona had somehow missed her.

Mona emptied a clip, hitting all around Candy and was loading a fresh clip when, wham!...a shot was fired from directly behind her. It was Molly. The Winchester had found its mark, and a well-aimed hunting round tore into the middle of Mona's back, breaking her spine and blowing a chunk of bone and flesh out a large hole in her chest. She was thrown to the ground by the impact of the 30-30 hollow point bullet.

CHAPTER TWENTY-SEVEN

In a Pig's Eye

CANDY GOT UP and walked over to Mona, who was shuddering with pain, curled up on the ground. She saw Ashur's body nearby.

"Is this all of you scumbags?" she said.

Mona looked up, obviously in horrible pain, and said, "Yes, we've failed. Kill me. Please kill me!"

Candy said, "I'd be happy to, but not just yet." Molly had seen it all and had gone for the truck. In just a few minutes, she pulled in next to Candy. Owen was awake, but had "one hell of a headache."

They loaded Ashur and Mona in the bed of the truck. They moved Fadia to the bed, as well, and put all the equipment in the front. Molly sat in the back with the Syrians, holding a Glock in her lap just in case any of them had enough life left to cause a problem.

Candy had gone off into the brush and picked up the dead pig. She put it in the bed of the truck. She also gathered up the rest of the weapons and the second suitcase.

She got into the truck and said, "Molly, if any of those bastards move the wrong way, kill them."

Candy got behind the wheel and drove down the gravel road to the highway. She pulled out onto the blacktop and crossed over onto the gravel service road. She looked over at Owen.

Candy said, "Owen, I've got one hell of an idea. Are you with me?"

Owen looked over at Candy. She had been though hell tonight. He didn't know for sure all she'd done, but it was evident she was in the driver's seat in more ways than one.

He said, "Candy, I'm with you. Do what you need to do. Where are we headed?"

Candy smiled. She drove across the blacktop.

"We need to pick up those other bastards' bodies. Help me find them. They drove around for twenty minutes before finding the shredded and broken body of Samir. They threw him in the back with the rest and drove over to the Hummer. Said's body was nearby and they picked it up.

"Now, we are going over to that dry well at the end of the service road...remember, the well we just capped? It will be easy to open up," she said coldly.

Candy drove the truck back onto the service road and took it all the way to the end. In a few minutes they were pulling up to the well site.

Candy said, "Come on, Owen. Molly, stay and watch them. Kill anything that moves."

Candy and Owen walked over to the capped well. She had brought along a crowbar and couple of wrenches and a large hammer from the truck. Owen finally understood ... but not all of it. After some degree of serious effort, they managed to remove the well cap. The open 32 inch pipe went down into the ground several hundred feet before it bottomed out in a cold pit of blackness.

Candy went back to the truck and grabbed hold of Mona's arm. She pulled her out of the bed of the truck, letting her hit the ground hard with a thud. Mona said something in Arabic.

"I'm sure," said Candy. She dragged the woman over to the well and unceremoniously shoved her head first into the hole. Mona screamed as Candy pushed her down with her foot. Mona slipped into the depths, screaming until she could no longer be heard. Her futile attempts at slowing her descent by scratching and clawing at the walls could be clearly heard ... for a very short while.

One by one, Candy pushed the rest of the intruders into the hole ... Fadia, Said, Samir, and finally Ashur. She went back to the truck and brought the dead pig over to the well. She threw the carcass down next to the well.

"You know what Moslems think about pork, don't you? They consider them to be the worst of all filth. She laughed and shoved the body of the Javalina down the hole. "How do you like your pork, you bastards!" she shouted down the well.

They worked a few minutes to re-cap the well. Candy cranked down the last few bolts on the iron plate.

"Let's go get the one by the road, now," she said. "Maybe he's dead, if he's lucky."

Molly and Owen watched silently as Candy pulled up to Bernardo. He was lying along side the road, still holding his stomach. He looked like he was still breathing. His clothing was covered in blood and dirt. He wasn't moving. Candy walked over to him and poked him with a stick of mesquite. Bernardo moaned, but didn't speak.

Candy turned to Molly and Owen and said, "Dammit, he's still alive. What do you guys want to do with this one?"

They all smiled. "Let's come back for him later," Molly said.

CHAPTER TWENTY-EIGHT

Finality

BEFORE THEY went back to the Club, they stopped near the Hummer to say goodbye to College Boy. Owen was the only one who would look inside of the still smoldering hulk of the SUV. He didn't linger. It was a horrible sight. He told the women that there wasn't much left, just a blackened body mostly turned to carbon. The young man's body was unrecognizable.

They drove silently back to the Girvin Social Club, arriving just as the storm ended and the sun was starting to rise. No sooner had they pulled into the parking lot, Janci wheeled her gold Lexus in behind them. She was followed closely by two Pecos County Sheriff vehicles, a Texas State Trooper, and several black Chevy Suburbans with dark tinted windows.

Candy, Molly and Owen stepped out of the truck. Molly grabbed hold of Owen's hand and held it tightly. They looked at one another, knowingly. Candy was crying quietly to herself, knowing her man was inside the Club. Janci led the crowd of law enforcement people up to the steps of the Club. The men from the Suburbans were in full battle gear, ready for action.

Meanwhile, down the road, Bernardo had managed to find the strength to get up. He made his way along the blacktop to the railroad tracks that ran a short distance from the Social Club, and walked slowly along them to distance himself from the commotion. He sat down, gingerly, next to a large rock by to the tracks and waited. The bleeding from his wounds had stopped, and he was exhausted and weak.

He was sure, from the wear on the steel, that there would likely be a train passing through, and he hoped it would be heading south.

As the sun rose, Bernardo noticed a large petroleum plant just a few miles to the north. They hadn't seen it in the darkness and storm last night, and it was so near. Bernardo's mind raced, and he thought to himself, They think this is over . . . . .

The End